Nick Trenton grew up as a farm boy in rural Illinois in USA. He obtained a BS in Economics, followed by an MA in Behavioral Psychology.

Nick likes to say that he has become a professional expert at one of his favorite hobbies: people-watching. He is an accomplished skier and dreams of travelling the world and hosting a food show like Anthony Bourdain. He currently lives in Chicago, Illinois.

Other titles by Nick Trenton,
published by Manjul/Amaryllis

the art of self-therapy

How to Grow, Gain Self-Awareness, & Understand Your Emotions

Nick Trenton

AMARYLLIS
An imprint of Manjul Publishing House

AMARYLLIS

An imprint of Manjul Publishing House Pvt. Ltd.
• C-16, Sector 3, Noida, Uttar Pradesh 201 301, India
Website: www.manjulindia.com

Registered Office:
• 2nd Floor, Usha Preet Complex, 42 Malviya Nagar,
Bhopal 462 003 – India

Distribution Centres
Ahmedabad, Bengaluru, Chennai, Hyderabad,
Kochi, Kolkata, Mumbai, Noida, Pune

The Art of Self-Therapy by Nick Trenton

This paperback edition first published in 2023
Sixth impression 2026

ISBN 978-93-5543-293-3

Printed and bound in India by Repro India Limited

Contents

PART 3

Thoughts Are the Code That Programs Your Life

PART 4

Build the Life You Want One Action at a Time

PART 1

Getting To Know Your Deeper Self

Therapy is a wonderful thing. A trained mental health professional can help you explore psychological blind spots, set goals, and work with you through tricky thought patterns so you can gently change them. But what if you don't want therapy, or can't access it?

"Self-therapy" is a way to recreate some of the benefits of conventional therapy, but on your own terms. This book is all about giving you the tools you need to gain better self-awareness, build emotional maturity, and learn to change your behavior so that you can start creating the kind of life you want for yourself.

The tools we'll explore in the chapters that follow are the very same ones used by cognitive behavioral therapists, counselors, and psychologists the world over. By adapting them for your own use, you can start cultivating more contentment with who you are, challenge limiting thought patterns, and zoom out to gain a broader view of the narratives on which your life is structured. From there, you can *consciously* choose what you want for your life, rather than passively being at the mercy of these forces.

In the pages that follow, we'll start at the very beginning: your deepest self. In Part 1, we'll look at helpful techniques and mindset shifts that will help you master self-exploration and gain deeper awareness into how you actually tick. Then, in Part 2, we'll take a look into the past and investigate how your family and early experiences shaped who you are today. After all, if you want to rewrite the story of your life, you need to understand the story as it is so far, and how it got that way.

In Part 3, we shift our attention to the cognitive manifestations of our core beliefs and inner emotional realities: our thoughts. Using evidence-based cognitive behavioral techniques, we'll look at our thought processes and take charge of them, asking whether they're genuinely helping us achieve the kind of life we want. Finally, once all this groundwork has been laid, we can dive into the practical work of Part 4, where we explore ways to start taking action and changing our behavior in the world day after day.

Self-therapy isn't learned overnight, and it can be challenging at times, but rest assured that no matter where you are now or where you want to be, these techniques will bring improvements to your life. Whether you are looking for more direction and purpose, want to improve your relationships, or simply need to get a handle on who you are and what you really want in life, there's something in this book for you. Let's jump in.

CHAPTER 1

What It Means To Master Self-Exploration

What you'll learn in this chapter: why and how to improve your self-awareness, as well as a six-part process for learning more about what makes you tick.

Here's a good question to begin with: WHO ARE YOU?

According to psychologist Dr. Tom Stevens, mastering self-exploration can provide us with a sophisticated, nuanced answer to this question.

But we cannot answer that question until we have something crucial: self-awareness. Too many people go through life on autopilot or in a kind of distracted haze. They are not really sure what they feel, what they want, or who they are. They are unclear about their values, have fuzzy boundaries, or have never really stopped to consider why they behave as they do.

If you've ever asked yourself . . .

"Why do I do that?"
"What do I really want?" or
"Why am I unhappy?"

. . . then chances are you can benefit from more self-exploration. When you have explored yourself in enough depth, you can identify who you are as a person (both strengths and weaknesses), take responsibility for what you need, and then make informed decisions about the choices you want to make in your life.

If you embark on any plan for personal development without self-awareness, though, you are merely going through the motions. Perhaps you end up doing what you think you "should" be doing, or substitute other people's desires and values for your own. Not only does self-awareness make you happier, more resilient, and more accepting of who you are, it also allows you to live authentically and create a life that is right for *you*.

So what exactly is self-exploration? According to Ryan Howes, PhD, psychologist, writer, and professor in Pasadena, California, it involves "taking a look at your own thoughts, feelings, behaviors, and motivations and asking **why**. It's looking for the roots of who we are."

The idea is that if you can understand why you do something, you empower yourself to do something different. If you don't truly understand what is going on in your heart and mind, you only have a dim hope of fulfilling your potential, overcoming obstacles, or connecting fully with others in your relationships.

Beginner Strategies: Make Self-Exploration a Habit

Self-awareness is like exercise—the more you practice, the better you become!

The best way to gain more self-awareness is to build it into your life as a regular, consistent habit. This can be as simple as asking yourself, whenever you remember, "What do I notice about myself right now?"

Simply pause, become aware, and *be* with yourself for a moment. Try just ten minutes to start (what about trying right now, as you read this book?). Notice if you get distracted and your mind wanders. Notice what you're feeling and where that experience sits in your body. Notice the thoughts in your mind. Notice what you're doing. Notice what came just before. Even notice thoughts like, "I'm bored. Am I doing it right?"

Unplug and check in with yourself. Importantly, you don't have to *do* anything about what you notice. You don't have to judge, interpret, cling to, avoid, or analyze what you notice. Just notice. For example, you might be having a shower and suddenly notice that you're in a really bad mood. Why? You pause and decide to become aware for a moment.

You sit somewhere quietly and notice that you're annoyed. You notice your thoughts and how they're rushing ahead to an imagined future encounter at work. You realize you were rehearsing a hypothetical argument in your mind. You notice how you're actually scowling a little, your jaw is tense, and you're not paying much attention to anything else. Without awareness, none of this would have been noticed. Let's take a closer look.

Tom Stevens' Six-Step Self-Exploration Process

Once you've gained some practice with the above exercise, you can challenge yourself to go further and follow Dr. Stevens' six-step approach for digging a little deeper.

Step 1: Switch on Your "Inner Noticer"

As we did in the previous exercise, just get into the habit of observing yourself neutrally and without judgment—like a scientist taking a step back and recording data from afar. See if you can notice thoughts, feelings, physical sensations, and actions—and the difference between them.

Example: You notice your bad mood in the shower, your tense jaw muscles, and the mini argument you seem to be holding in your head.

Step 2: Notice Any Problematic Situations?

This step may happen automatically, but see if any patterns begin to emerge.

> *What is the "problem" exactly?*
>
> *When did it start?*
>
> *What came before it?*

Does this sequence of events usually happen this way?

What typically comes after this experience?

What is going on in your environment when this happens?

Example: You realize, with repeated moments of awareness, that you actually feel this way most mornings, during most showers. You realize this may be a problem for you and is setting the day off on the wrong foot.

You look more closely at yourself for a few days and notice that you don't wake up irritable, but seem to feel that way only after your mind wanders in the shower and starts to entertain certain thoughts and "predictions."

Step 3: Notice the Strongest Emotions and Where They Lead

Notice not only what you feel but the intensity of those feelings. There may be some emotions that you become aware of that you are actually quite uncomfortable with. If you can notice that you are trying to resist or avoid them, see if you can keep maintaining awareness anyway. In fact, become most curious about the strongest, most difficult, or most uncomfortable emotions.

Keep asking more questions of this emotion—what came before? What happened next?

Example: The strongest emotion, even though you try to avoid it, turns out to be *anger*. You say you're annoyed and find yourself blaming random occurrences that come after your shower, but the more awareness you bring to the situation, the more you see that you are in fact very angry at something. What? This is difficult to admit because you don't consider yourself an angry person. But you keep being aware.

Step 4: Try To Notice Any Emerging Connections

Now's the time to really put on your scientist cap and bravely investigate those strong feelings, rather than avoid or deny them.

> *What images, ideas, thoughts, or memories seem to most often be connected with the strong emotion?*
>
> *What strengthens these emotions and what seems to make them fade?*
>
> *Can you connect this experience or emotion with something similar in the past?*
>
> *If there are many situations that produce this emotion, what do those situations have in common? What connects them?*

Example: You are aware that you keep rehearsing imaginary conversations in your mind, where you envision your work colleagues are criticizing you, and you are angrily defending yourself, as well as venting off a long list of hidden resentments of your own.

In these conversations, you find yourself saying things like, "Oh, so I suppose you think you're perfect, then?" and, "If you're such an expert, then why do you pay me to do it for you, huh?" In time, you notice that this reminds you of something very interesting: the way you feel is very similar to arguments you used to have with your father growing up, where he would criticize your work no matter how hard you tried.

Step 5: What Is the Underlying Core Belief, Value, or Theme Behind This Emotion?

Keep going and you should eventually uncover the bigger picture that connects everything together—thought, feelings, behavior. The magic of self-awareness is this ability to see the overarching patterns and themes that are playing out in your life.

You've become aware of all the surface details; now, what is the bigger underlying theme that brings them all together? In what ways are all the separate issues you're experiencing alike?

Example: You realize that the bigger picture is that you're feeling insecure about your performance at work and are assuming that people are judging you. You play out imaginary conversations in your own mind, but this is not an accurate reflection of what is actually happening in your workplace right now, but an echo of something from your deeper childhood.

Step 6: Use Your Insights To Identify Your Boundaries, Then Take Control

Self-awareness is not just something we do for the sake of it. It's something we develop and then *put to use*. Once you've gained greater insight into your problem, there's one of two ways forward:

1. Identify the external cause of the problem and take responsibility for acting, given what we know
2. Identify the inner cause of the problem (i.e., us!) and take responsibility for that, whether that means changing our thoughts, emotions, or behaviors.

As you can see, in both options, we need to own up to our portion of the problem and take responsibility for acting in our own best interests. After all, self-awareness that doesn't lead to any concrete changes in the real world is not much more than navel-gazing!

Example: You ask yourself honestly if there's any objective reason to believe that people are critical of you at work. When you're content there aren't, you deliberately choose to become aware any time you catch yourself getting stuck in imaginary "replay" conversations. Then, you rehearse a mantra: "I'm competent and capable, and I'm doing the best I can. I am proud of myself."

Now, the above example may seem insignificant on the surface, but imagine if such a problem was allowed to run its course without ever being revealed by the light of awareness. You may have gotten out of the shower *every single morning* in a bad mood, never really knowing why. Maybe one day you went into work feeling grumpy and sensitive and snapped at a colleague, assuming they were being rude. This could set off a whole cascade of negative outcomes—all of which could be avoided if you knew yourself better.

On the other hand, while this is happening, other things are *not* happening: You are not giving yourself the opportunity to fix the real problem, which is the unresolved issues you have with your father and with your own sense of self-worth. Maybe you even assume the problem is that you feel angry "for no reason," so you start trying to solve the problem in all the wrong ways—i.e., reading a self-help book about anger or taking up Tai Chi.

These things are great, but they probably won't work because they are not addressing the real root of your problem, which is more accurately low self-esteem. This is why it's so important to start with awareness and self-exploration as the first step.

Becoming aware is a simple, free, and easy thing that any of us can do right now, in this moment.

As our example shows, what started out as simply curiosity and awareness of the most ordinary daily activities can yield valuable insight into who you are as a person. All that's needed is time, patience, and the willingness to know ourselves better. In the chapters that follow, we'll be taking this foundation of self-exploration and awareness and building on it as we go.

CHAPTER 2

Take a Walk on the Dark Side With Shadow Work

What you'll learn in this chapter: what the shadow is and how and why to embrace it with acceptance and compassion.

When most people experience uncomfortable emotions, they want to do one thing and one thing only: get away from them. In fact, they may turn to therapy with precisely this attitude: "Make it go away!"

However, this is the opposite of the mindset you need. As we saw above, what's required is a willingness to tolerate, accept, and be with emotions, **all our emotions**, no matter how uncomfortable they are and without judgment.

If you start to make awareness and self-exploration a bigger part of your life, sooner or later you're going to encounter parts of yourself that you really, really don't like. And your tendency will be to run as far away from them as possible! However, this is where the technique of shadow work comes into play.

Carl Jung was the psychiatrist, author, and theorist who first introduced the idea of the shadow. In simple terms, the shadow is our psychological blind spot—it contains everything that we can't "see"—i.e., that is outside our awareness. Every person has a shadow, but the idea is that if we can acknowledge it, accept it, and integrate it back into our awareness as something that rightly belongs to us, we enjoy greater mental health, authenticity, creativity, energy, and maturity.

When we are young, we have certain experiences that teach us that some parts of ourselves are acceptable and others aren't. In order to survive in the world and get our needs met, we unconsciously decide to disown those "bad" parts of ourselves and disidentify with them. We push them out of awareness.

For example, our parents may tell us that our anger is bad and punish us when we yell or express frustration. So, we put "anger" into the shadow. It hasn't gone anywhere, but we don't see it anymore.

This "dark side" of our conscious awareness doesn't contain just bad things, by the way. We can also disconnect from and disown positive feelings, attributes, or thoughts. We may put into the shadow things like excitement, hope, silliness, and so on because of early experiences that taught us these things were bad.

So what's the problem? Isn't it a good thing to section off the worst parts of ourselves? The trouble is that the shadow is never completely hidden. It still shows itself; however, it may do so in sneaky ways. Our shadow may express itself in strange behaviors we don't understand—in dreams, in slips of the tongue, or in behavior others can see but we don't ourselves recognize.

Perhaps our anger comes out in passive aggressiveness. We may say, "I'm the least angry person in the world!" Yet somehow, others can *feel* the anger radiating off us anyway. It's because it's still there, in the shadow. As long as we have a shadow, we will remain at least partly unconscious of our deeper motivations and may be trapped in behaviors that are not good for us, without really understanding why.

On top of this, there's a sneaky phenomenon called projection, in which we end up incorrectly ascribing to others the feelings and thoughts we ourselves have but have disowned and relegated to the shadow. The classic example is the person who is being dishonest but has pushed that fact out of awareness. The shadow seeps out, however, in the form of them constantly accusing *others* of hiding something or being dishonest. They're projecting when they say, "The problem isn't in me, it's in you!"

In this way, what we are unconscious of can harm us. It can threaten our relationships, jeopardize our work, and weaken our potential. It can also leave us confused, immature, and fragile people who lack wisdom and self-knowledge. The solution? Again, it's awareness! According to Jung, **we improve our lives and heal when we integrate the shadow.**

That may sound like a good idea, but nobody wants to look at their shadow. Nobody wants to face up to the things they cannot face in themselves, by definition! So how exactly do we see what we can't see?

Accepting the Shadow

First things first, what you *don't* want to do is continue to judge and condemn the "bad" parts of yourself—after all, this is precisely what caused it to be shoved out of awareness in the first place. No, we cannot be whole and integrate the shadow by heaping on more scorn or shame. Instead, we need to be curious, compassionate, and open-minded.

To engage our shadow, we need a few things:

- Patience
- A genuinely accepting and nonjudgmental attitude
- Honesty
- The willingness to be brave enough to face things we don't like about ourselves

Here are a few ways to do that.

Technique 1: Pay Attention to Your Emotional Reactions

Imagine someone has a drinking problem that they can't quite admit to themselves. In their shadow is everything they deny about themselves: a lack of self-control, frequent reckless behavior, even the habit of denial itself. They are unwilling to face up to the fact that they behave in ways they don't like when they drink too much, and unwilling to accept the shame they feel because of it. In fact, they could go for years never acknowledging this problem.

One day, this person notices themselves feeling extremely judgmental about a friend who smokes marijuana. They say, "It's totally irresponsible. Don't they care about what they're doing to their health? So reckless. They obviously lack self-control! I'm so disappointed in them . . ." Others might be puzzled at this outburst. Why such a strong reaction?

The answer probably lies in the person's shadow. Read through their thoughts again, and you'll see that this is in fact what they think of *themselves.* The shadow can hide from awareness, but it often shows itself as judgment of others, or strong and disproportionate reactions that don't quite fit the situation at hand.

It's a good idea to become aware of anything that seems to "push your buttons" and cause a reaction that is bigger than it should be. Prick your ears if you seem to have been "triggered" automatically by something, and become curious why. What bothers you in others is often something you've disowned in yourself!

Technique 2: Embrace Imperfection

While rage, jealousy, and lust are all understandably relegated to the shadow, much of what we put there isn't really so bad when you think about it. The shadow may feel big and scary and overwhelming, but it's often like the monster under the bed—when you peek to check, there's nothing there.

If you can learn to embrace flaws and imperfection and accept that **you are a complex person with both good and bad qualities**, then you weaken the power of the shadow. One way to do this is to consciously decide you will judge and condemn others less often (hint: to the extent you judge them, you also judge yourself). Another idea is to deliberately ask, "What's so wrong with being a flawed human being?"

Here's an exercise to try.

1. Identify the attributes, ideas, thoughts, or feelings you most often judge in others.
2. Write them down ("I hate stupid people").
3. Now rephrase the sentences so they apply to you ("I can be stupid sometimes").
4. Read through these new sentences and notice how you feel. Ask yourself, is it *really* the end of the world if they're true? Does it mean that you're not worthy of love, or that you don't also possess good qualities? You may notice that the more forgiving you are about other people's stupid mistakes, the easier it is to accept occasional stupidity in yourself, and vice versa.
5. If you're having trouble, try to imagine a loved one who has that attribute, yet whom you still adore and respect anyway (maybe you realize that your pet Labrador is the stupidest being on the planet, but that doesn't stop them from also being the one you love most!). Imagine that you, too, are perfectly acceptable as you are, warts and all.

Technique 3: Ask for Feedback

Your shadow is a bit like the back of your head—you can't see it, but it may be very visible to everyone else!

Asking someone you trust and respect to help you see your blind spots takes some courage, but it's well worth it. Identify someone who you believe knows you well—the last thing you want is to ask someone who will accidentally project their own shadow onto you! Ask someone who themselves has been able to demonstrate emotional maturity, and who will be happy to help you look objectively at your shadow without bringing judgment into the equation.

Since this may be a tall order, another option is to enlist the help of a therapist, counselor, or psychologist to help you work through the more sensitive parts of your shadow. They'll be able to hold you accountable while keeping a "safe space" that won't trigger more defensiveness in you.

If both of these options are not feasible, you can always sit down and carefully consider the feedback you've already received from others. Can you find any themes or patterns in what you've been told by ex-partners, old bosses (or current ones!), friends, family members, or even random people? You may already have been given heaps of feedback that consistently points to your shadow, only you haven't been courageous enough to take it fully on board.

Notice if you repeatedly find yourself angry with people's appraisals of who you are (again, it's about noticing *disproportionate* reactions) and ask honestly if they may have a point. Think back to disagreements you may have had or recall criticisms or advice others may have repeatedly given you. You may have dismissed it in the past, but could it be that others have said similar things? Could there be a pattern?

The important thing about shadow work is that you are not trying to play "gotcha!" You are not attempting to catch yourself out or punish yourself. If on reflection you notice that more than a handful of people have mentioned how over the top you can be at times, just own and acknowledge that. Avoid getting lost in shame or embarrassment about it—just accept it gracefully and be proud of yourself that you're able to be aware.

If that fails, one technique always works: humor. Laugh at yourself a little. "Oh, there I go again! What a drama llama I am. How do you put up with me?"

CHAPTER 3

Gestalt Techniques—Be Present, Be Responsible, Be Whole

What you'll learn in this chapter: how to open yourself more fully to the present by putting the past to rest.

As you embark on more self-exploration and become more aware of yourself in the present, you may notice something interesting: that so much of your experience is actually all about the **past**.

Gestalt therapy is a kind of psychotherapy first introduced by Fritz and Laura Perls in the 1940s and addresses this issue of "letting go of the past."

You may start to notice that what keeps you from living in the present or planning for the future is the fact that you have unresolved conflicts and patterns that are living on from the past. Gestalt therapy, then, is all about healing that past so you can focus on the present moment and your responsibilities in that moment. If you can do that, the theory goes, you can make better decisions and greatly improve your resilience, self-knowledge, and well-being.

In a 2018 *Good Therapy* article on Gestalt principles, licensed counselor Jodi Clarke puts it this way: "Gestalt therapy is a humanistic, holistic, person-centered form of psychotherapy that is focused on an individual's present life and challenges rather than delving into past experiences." The idea is not to endlessly rehash the past, but to *resolve* and *release* it so we are free to take responsibility for our lives right now.

What do we need to begin Gestalt therapy techniques? As you might have guessed, it's awareness.

First, let's look at this word "gestalt," which is a German term that roughly translates to "whole." Its meaning suggests that "the whole is greater than the sum of the parts." A gestalt is then the meaningful form or shape that we give to all our collected experiences. **With our perception, we make sense of the world with our narrative and our identity—this is a gestalt.**

However, every person is connected to and influenced by their environment and others. So, it follows, then, that if we want to understand ourselves and fulfil our potential, we need to also understand our context. To change, we have to become aware of what is, and also accept it. In this way, we relieve suffering and anxiety and free ourselves to seek growth and development instead.

Gestalt therapists believe the reason we are unhappy in life is because there is a gap between our present and our future. In other words, our mind may travel faster and further into the future than the concrete circumstances of our lives can keep up with! Thus, we create worry, anticipation, and a whole world of expectations and interpretations that cause us trouble. We also cause ourselves trouble when we use our minds to travel back to the past.

But here, the Perls have some advice: *all we can ever experience is the present.* The perception we have of the past or the future is not "objective" because it is actually a reflection of how we're living right now.

So far so good, but how can we apply any of these insights into our own lives? Below, we'll look at five popular Gestalt therapy strategies that you can try for yourself.

Strategy 1: Pending Issues

A pending issue is an event in the past that continues to have an influence on the present. These issues are like knots, blocks, or mismanaged perceptions that linger—for example, a grudge against a family member or an unresolved issue with an old friend. According to the Perls, we resolve these issues by engaging them and refusing to avoid them anymore. We need to construct an imaginary encounter in which we face this issue now, in the present, and put it to bed.

Maybe we say a final farewell to someone who died before we could share what we wanted to. Maybe we address an unspoken resentment or ask someone for forgiveness.

How? Close your eyes and go quiet within yourself, then mentally evoke the person, issue, or event. Don't flee any uncomfortable emotions. Do what you need to do to "close the circle." We'll look at this idea in more detail when we talk about "re-parenting the inner child," but for now, just rehearse in your imagination any act or words that will help you find closure.

Strategy 2: Addressing the Empty Chair

This is a familiar technique, but some people aren't aware that it comes from Gestalt therapy. Here, you take your mental and emotional perception of a person or event and **externalize** it so you can then engage with it or have a dialogue. This gets unresolved issues moving again and allows trapped feelings to be acknowledged and then released.

For example, you may imagine that your childhood bully is sitting in the chair opposite you. Really visualize them there, and now imagine everything you wish you had said back then. Speak your mind.

Or you may picture an ex-partner in the chair, and by talking to them, you play out your mourning for that relationship so your emotions can be released. It can be more abstract than this, though. Put your fear itself into the chair and personify it. What does it want? What is it telling you? More importantly, what do you have to say to it?

On the other hand, if you're feeling anxious and afraid, you could also put your strength into the chair and talk to that. Ask what it needs to be stronger. Ask why it's hiding away right now and letting fear take over.

As you can see, there is a lot of flexibility and creativity in how you use this technique! Just remember that the goal is to bring the past into the present so you can actively process it, engage with it, and release it.

Strategy 3: "I'm Responsible"

When you are burdened with past issues, you are really absolving yourself of the responsibility to live dynamically and spontaneously in the present.

If we can become aware of and accept our own duty to the present, however, we can start embracing our responsibility and begin making conscious, proactive choices. In other words, we make the shift from, "This is who I am/was," to, "Who do I want to be right now?"

There are a few phrases, mantras, or ways of speaking that will help put you into the responsible, present-focused mindset:

> "I'm responsible for that."
>
> "I accept that it's my job to change things."
>
> "I have a choice in what happens next."

For example, you may find that you're wracked with guilt and shame about how you behaved in the past. You may be carrying that embarrassment and regret around with you, but by doing so, you only limit your ability to make good decisions right now, in the present.

Using the "I'm responsible" strategy, you teach

yourself to say, "I can't change the past, but I am in charge of what I do and say now, and I choose to do better." Just remember to make sure your responsibility is anchored in the only place that you genuinely have it: the present.

Strategy 4: Continuum of Consciousness

This technique is about shifting focus from the WHY of your experience to the HOW.

> *How* are you responding to life's challenges, experiences, and problems?
>
> *How* does it feel?
>
> *How* are you personally carrying this experience?

Too often, we allow our self-exploration quest to be dominated by the question, "Why is this happening?"

But this question can only take you so far. Asking "how" questions actually gives you deeper insight into the unique ways that your experience is unfolding **for you**. No psychological theory can tell you what that is. No amount of reading about other people's experiences will give you a true understanding of your own.

So, before you leap in with "why?" take the time to simply observe and be curious about "how?" Flesh out your experience. Describe it. Take a moment to really perceive what that feels like. For some people, their experiences are better grasped by imagery, metaphor, poems, art, or other non-verbal expressions.

Strategy 5: Change Questions into Affirmations

This is a technique that will help you firm up your internal reality and get you into the proactive, responsible mindset. It's a simple but powerful approach.

Take your questions and turn them into affirmative, true statements. For example, one day you become aware of yourself thinking, "Why do I feel so depressed today?" So, you convert it to: "I feel depressed today."

That's not all, though. Once you definitively make this statement, follow it up with responsible, proactive behavior in the present. Embrace how you feel and face up to it, but then move on, asking what you can do about it right now. "I feel depressed today, so I'm going to go for a walk in the sunshine and make sure I get an early night tonight."

As you can see, there is the brave acknowledgment of your present reality, as well as the commitment to taking action—again, in the present reality. If you keep dwelling on questions ("What's wrong with me? Why did she say that? Why am I having so much trouble right now?"), you are actually trapping yourself in a state of mind that exacerbates your suffering rather than addresses it. It's passive, and it encourages a victim mindset.

On the other hand, in stating something outright, you might actually convince yourself of how inaccurate it is. In this case, you can consciously choose to let the statement go and refuse to have it take up any more room in your mind. "Why do I suck at everything I try?

I suck at everything I try. Oh wait, that does sound a bit dramatic. I haven't succeeded at this thing yet, but I take responsibility, and I'm going to keep practicing without getting discouraged." In this way, emotions and perceptions are kept alive and flowing rather than left to stagnate passively. Think of it as a way to constantly refresh and update yourself into the present so you are not bogged down by useless thoughts that go nowhere.

CHAPTER 4

Understanding Internal Family Systems

What you'll learn in this chapter: that there are many parts of you, but well-being occurs when all those parts find a way to live together.

In reading the above technique, you may have noticed that there were seemingly *two* versions of yourself, and these two were in dialogue:

One part of you was critical, stuck in the past, and acting on autopilot.

The other part was wiser, kinder, and able to step in with a more objective rebuttal.

This theme is expanded on in Internal Family Systems, or IFS. The idea is that **everyone is made of several smaller subpersonalities—i.e., the mind is like a mini family.** This means we can talk about and deal with the different inner parts of ourselves in much the same way as we would with a literal family. The roles of each of these parts are not set in stone; we can evolve and change. IFS therapy, then, is about bringing all your separate parts together to work as a whole.

IFS was first introduced by family therapist Richard Schwartz. He described the patterns he noticed in his patients: "What I heard repeatedly were descriptions of what they often called their 'parts'—the conflicted subpersonalities that resided within them." He set about trying to understand these parts as well as how they related to one another. If the mind is a family, what does a "happy family" look like?

The theory states that there are probably infinite aspects within each person, but they tend to fall into three main groups:

Firefighter – These are protectors who step in to help when triggered, i.e., "put out the fire" in whatever way possible (healthy and sustainable or not!).

Manager – Manages emotions and situations via planning and control.

Exile – The exile is basically what both the managers and firefighters are working to contain. The exile's job is to hold difficult feelings of shame, pain, or hurt from previous unresolved experiences.

These parts of us all have a purpose. Even the "bad parts"! When you work with an IFS therapist, your goal is to find out what that purpose is.

As an example, you may have experienced a trauma in your childhood that created feelings of anger and rage in you. These feelings are exiled when the manager steps in to suppress and contain them. Furthermore, when these feelings of rage and anger do break free, the firefighter is ready to step in and manage the emergency. This may be in the form of addictive behaviors that numb and distract, or projection onto someone else so that you don't have to face the exile too closely.

An IFS therapist will typically walk you through a six-part process, but you can replicate the same thing on your own:

Step 1: Find

As with so many of the techniques we'll discuss in this book, begin by becoming aware. Notice all sensations, as well as how your body and mind are connected. Perhaps you notice a tightness in your stomach.

Step 2: Focus

Instead of avoiding or fleeing these sensations, put your focus more intently on them. Notice this feeling of stomach tightness, for example, without letting your mind wander somewhere else.

Step 3: Flesh Out

Once you have sustained attention on a sensation or a part of yourself, try to expand on it.

What emotions are connected to it? Do any other ideas or associations come to mind? For example, maybe you realize that this stomach tightness feels a little like anxiety, but a particular kind of anxiety. Maybe certain colors and images spring to mind, or you imagine a person, symbol, or image that embodies this specific sensation.

Step 4: Feel Toward

Become aware of how you feel toward this fleshed-out sensation. What kind of a role does it play in your life? How do you respond? Maybe you notice that this is a regular sensation for you, and that when it comes up, you tend to panic and do what you can to ignore it or distract yourself.

Step 5: Befriend

Here's where the hardest work happens: instead of ignoring or distracting yourself, you decide to get to know this part better.

Imagine it literally is a long-lost friend or estranged family member you are welcoming back into your life. Now, you don't have to embrace it or pretend that it feels better than it does. All you have to do is see it, acknowledge it, and accept it for what it is. Also, accepting it doesn't mean you necessarily want that feeling to stay there forever!

Step 6: Explore Your Fear

Many of these parts of us are there for one reason: fear. So now, ask this part of yourself: "What are you afraid will happen if you're not here?" Try to imagine what this part of yourself is trying to achieve, and what role its presence plays for you. Maybe you notice that this anxious knot in your stomach is actually, in its own strange way, trying to protect you.

What this six-step process does is normalize your reactions and bring them all together as one. IFS has much in common with Gestalt therapy since it's all about holistic wellbeing. It also relates to Jung's shadow work because in engaging the different parts of ourselves, we are re-claiming previously disinherited aspects with acceptance and compassion.

IFS therapy works because it encourages awareness and invites us to look at ourselves with kindness and as *wholes.* Also, instead of pathologizing parts of ourselves, we accept them and become curious.

What role is this part playing? If we can understand its purpose, we can choose to fulfil that purpose in a healthier, more conscious way. We can say, "Thank you, stomach pain, for trying to keep me safe, but there is nothing to fear."

Finally, IFS is a great way to deepen body-mind connection, and so may help with issues like chronic pain or the physical sides of depression and anxiety. That's because rather than seeing any sensation as a problem, we simply embrace it and welcome it into the "family"!

Here are a few more things to keep in mind:

- As you become aware, try personifying parts of yourself and literally asking, "Who needs attention right now?"
- Often, "reactive" parts of us (i.e., those acting up with pain or unpleasant sensations) simply need validation and attention. You don't necessarily have to **do** anything, just **be with** the feeling.
- Set aside judgment by continually asking what this part's "job" is. How did it get that job (i.e., what early experiences brought it into being)? If it didn't have to do this job, what would it prefer to do instead? What would happen if it stopped doing its job?

These kinds of questions may feel a little corny at first, but they can be powerful. You may find out, for example, that, "If I let go of this fear, I'm afraid everything will go wrong," or, "It's my job to keep the other parts safe by controlling everything."

And so here we arrive at the three types again. The managers and firefighters will typically work hard to keep the exile at bay. For example, part of you may be sincerely depressed and hopeless, but another part is valiantly trying to put on a brave face and not let on how scared the other parts feel.

In other words, the parts of yourself are *in relationship*. One part of you may be trying to manage the others, a second part may be hiding away in shame, and a third part may be trying to pull everything together.

The goal of IFS is not to eliminate these different parts of yourself and pick the winner. Rather, it's the same goal as conventional family therapy: to get all the parts working in healthy, happy harmony. Some parts may release on their own once they realize they are no longer needed, or they may evolve and update, but this is not because they have been shunned or forced out of awareness.

The IFS model doesn't see people as just a mess of different sub-personalities, though. There is a Core Self at the center of it all, and in fact, it's this part that recognizes the existence of the other parts, observing and identifying certain triggers and reactions and consciously deciding to be more productive and more accepting.

The healthy, balanced Core Self is

- Confident
- Calm
- Creative
- Clear
- Curious
- Courageous
- Compassionate
- Connected
- Present
- Patient
- Persistent
- Playful

- Able to have perspective

To the extent that you are able to feel the above is the extent to which your Core Self is developed, and the degree to which you are consciously engaging with the present. Our goal with IFS, then, is to

1. Free certain parts of ourselves from extreme and unproductive roles
2. Rekindle trust in our Core Self
3. Harmonize all parts of ourselves in awareness and acceptance so they can work as a whole

If all of this sounds complicated, it needn't be. We can use this model any time we become aware of a difficult or unpleasant sensation. Turning inward, we can ask, *What part of me is this? What is its function?*

Then go from there. How you do that is up to you. You could keep a journal or combine this approach with some of the techniques already discussed above, especially the empty chair technique. You could draw a diagram illustrating your different aspects, or even play around with creating dialogues between all the parts—as you do so, you are strengthening your Core Self.

As you can imagine, IFS isn't appropriate for those who are dealing with delusions, psychosis, or schizophrenia, for obvious reasons. If you find that engaging with the separate parts of yourself is an overwhelming, threatening, or just plain weird idea, then give it a miss. There are plenty of alternative techniques to try.

Takeaways

- No matter who you are, it is possible to improve your life with the same evidence-based techniques used by cognitive behavioral therapists all over the world, i.e., self-therapy can help you live the life you want to live.
- Begin with asking who you are—that is, engaging in self-exploration. With practice, the habit of asking, "What do I notice about myself right now?" will become easier.
- Use Dr. Tom Stevens' six-step approach for cultivating self-exploration: 1) turn on your "inner noticer" and observe yourself without judgment, 2) zoom in on "the problem", 3) follow the strongest emotion, 4) allow yourself to notice any emerging patterns or overarching themes, 5) see what core beliefs are linking everything together, and 6) use these insights to inspire new, more conscious behavior.
- Carl Jung was the first to talk about the shadow, which is an archetype containing all the unconscious and disowned parts of our psyche. We reintegrate the shadow with patience, non-judgmental acceptance, honesty, and the willingness to face our dark side. We can do this by noticing disproportionate emotional reactions that may hint at the shadow's presence, mindfully embrace our imperfections and weaknesses (humor helps), as well as ask others for their

honest feedback on what we can't see in ourselves.

- Gestalt therapy is about understanding how your perception shapes your world, as well as releasing the past so you are more fully available to respond to the present. Some ways to do this include 1) rehearse acts of closure, 2) try the empty chair technique, 3) claim responsibility for your life, 4) shift from the WHY of your experience to the HOW, 5) change questions into affirmations.
- Internal Family Systems posits that the mind is made of many parts in relationship: firefighters, managers, and exiles. Befriend and feel into difficult emotions and normalize them by asking the role they play in your life.

PART 2

So, How Did You Get Here?

As you practice growing your self-awareness, as you engage your shadow and bring it into the light, and as you use various Gestalt techniques to strengthen your conscious living in the moment, you may start to encounter something ironic. You may discover that increasing awareness in the present tends to show you just how much is unresolved and unacknowledged in the past!

In Part 2, we expand our awareness to take a broader view of our context, our history, and all those early life experiences that shaped the people we are today. Again, the goal is not to dwell or to passively bemoan everything that went wrong. Rather, we are looking to understand, with a purpose to rewrite, release, or even challenge those early experiences.

Let's begin by considering one of the biggest influences on the way we think: the earliest bond we developed with our primary caregivers.

CHAPTER 5

What Is Your Attachment Style?

What you'll learn in this chapter: how your attachment style influences everything in your life, how to identify it, and how to work around it as a conscious, proactive adult in the present.

It's not a surprise that our environment and the formative relationships of our childhood years play a big part in who we are as adults. Yes, it is our responsibility to face ourselves as we are, warts and all, in the present. But you've also probably wondered more than once, "Where did all of this come from?"

Before we embark on questions of early childhood attachment and the inner child, we should note one important caveat: we seek to understand our childhoods not so we can blame others, get trapped in pessimism, or dwell in perpetual victimhood. We seek to understand so that we can reclaim conscious, responsible control over ourselves in the present.

British psychologist John Bowlby was the first to pioneer the theory of attachment styles. For him, the attachment bond is the emotional connection you develop with a primary caregiver—usually your mother. **The nature of this bond serves as an early template or model, influencing all other relationships you have in your life**. It becomes the single biggest influence for how you handle intimacy as an adult—and it's on a physiological level, too, since the infant's developing brain will literally take shape to adapt to the environment it finds itself in.

People's attachment styles vary according to what they've learned in those early relationships to caregivers. The idea is that if you had a stable, caring, and responsive bond with your caregiver, you developed a **secure attachment style**. When a caregiver responds to a helpless child's nonverbal cues for their needs to be met, those children grow up to be confident, self-aware, trusting, and able to form good relationships with others.

Other characteristics and behaviors resulting from secure attachment include:

- Empathy skills
- Good boundaries
- High self-worth
- More satisfying relationships
- Good communication skills
- The ability to express needs honestly

- Trust
- Ability to be alone, but valuing connection
- Mature, able to manage conflict and bounce back from disappointments

You don't need perfect care one hundred percent of the time to have formed a secure attachment. Similarly, just because you are securely attached doesn't mean you never experience relationship difficulties.

Without consistently responsive caregiving, however, you would develop an **insecure attachment style**. This is characterized by difficulties around intimacy, and connections that are too distant, too clingy, too anxious, or a little of all of these—hence too chaotic!

There are three main types of insecure attachment:

1. *Ambivalent*

Also called "anxious," this attachment style is characterized by neediness, uncertainty, and low self-esteem. Intimacy is desired, but there is a constant fear that others don't want to provide it. This is the person who can't help but worry whether their partner loves them, and is often embarrassed by their own clinginess.

Such a person may make their partners the center of their world and have difficulty trusting them or letting them have their own space, feeling that the distance provokes panic. They may have trouble with boundaries and feel worthless unless validated in a relationship. They may be jealous or even manipulative, or simply ask for constant reassurance.

The reason makes sense: this person's early caregiver relationship was inconsistent, which means the child learned to be anxious, never quite knowing if their needs would be met or not.

2. *Avoidant-Dismissive*

This style, however, is the opposite. People with this attachment style don't crave intimacy but resist it, feeling that closeness is threatening, so they'd prefer to meet their own needs and never rely on others. These are the people who value their independence, but they can feel claustrophobic in relationships and so uncomfortable with emotions (their own and others') that they appear cold and aloof.

Such a person may prefer shallow, fleeting connections where they can maintain their freedom, and they may cause damage when they dismiss others' emotions or even are unfaithful. As much as they resist it, they may still pine for connection but not know how to initiate it.

Their early caregiver relationship was one where they felt rejected. Rather than inconsistent care, there was very little care at all. This means that such a child would have been forced to intentionally disconnect to protect themselves, self-soothing with the idea that they could meet their own needs instead.

3. Disorganized or Chaotic

If your early caregiver relationship was abusive, traumatic, or neglectful, you may develop complex feelings around relationships, and even believe that you are undeserving of love or intimacy. You might not have had your needs met, yet still not have learned to meet them yourself, so your world and the people in it can feel unsafe and unpredictable.

Such a person may find relationships distressing and confusing and swing from one extreme to the next. They may experience addiction and show other destructive behaviors like aggression, violence, or drug use. They may deeply crave connection but violently push it away when it happens, alternatively controlling or feeling controlled. Relationships for those with disorganized attachment styles can feel scary and disorienting.

In each of the three styles above, the initial relationship echoes into adulthood. A person may have a mix of styles, and importantly, it's not about a caregiver's behavior so much as the infant's *perception* of that behavior.

Knowing all this, how can we use attachment theory to improve our own lives?

The first step is to identify what attachment style you might have. Then, crucially, realize that this can change—you are not doomed to stay that way forever! The more you understand about how your relationship mindset came to be, the more you can empower yourself to take steps to correct it. Here are some simple ideas.

Tip 1: Become Aware of Your Nonverbal Communication Patterns

Our earliest communication with our primary caregivers was nonverbal. Whenever you interact with others, you are (unconsciously) replicating that same dynamic in your gestures, tone, eye contact, and word choice.

You can immediately improve your relationships with others by consciously paying attention to the unconscious messages you may be sending. The next time you enter a conversation, deliberately relax and open your body, take deep belly breaths, and smile. It makes an enormous difference!

Tip 2: Develop Your Emotional Intelligence

The good news is that by applying some of the techniques in this book, developing your emotional intelligence is precisely what you're doing. Emotional intelligence, or EQ, is the ability to understand and regulate your own emotions so that you can empathize, communicate, and manage conflict. Improving your EQ will take a lifetime, but you can take a few easy first steps by making sure you are being present in every interaction you have with others.

Go calm and quiet in yourself and bring awareness to what is actually going on in an interaction. Truly listen. Bring your focus to everything the other person is communicating, not just the words they're saying. Notice how you feel in response. The start of any emotionally intelligent response is simply to have the presence of mind to ask, "What is going on with me emotionally right now? What about the other person?"

Tip 3: Find a Role Model

Sometimes, secure attachment is easier to feel than it is to understand. If you befriend people who have a secure attachment style, you can learn from them, modeling your behavior based on theirs. If you try to relate to someone who is also insecurely attached, then you can both destabilize one another and cause more pain and confusion. But a securely attached person can regulate and calm the interaction.

It may take a little time, but a securely attached partner or friend can gradually show you what it means to trust, to have boundaries, to accept with compassion, and so on. It's so much easier to spot your own unhelpful patterns of behavior if it's in the context of a normal, safe relationship. Alternatively, you might decide that for this issue, seeking a therapist or other mentor can help you "practice" what it means to live as someone who is comfortable and competent with intimacy.

Tip 4: Challenge Yourself

Finally, if you are aware that you have certain tendencies in relationships, you can consciously choose to challenge yourself to do something different. If you know that you have issues with trust, for example, ask if you can push yourself to go out of your comfort zone and trust anyway, just to see what happens. Pay attention to the result and then adjust. In this way, you construct behavioral experiments that teach you to test out different mindsets (we'll cover more on behavioral experiments in a later chapter).

All humans need and crave healthy connections with others, but our early experiences can interfere with the way we seek out, maintain, and provide intimacy with others. This doesn't just apply to romantic relationships. Any connection we have to other human beings, in any capacity, is a reflection of our attachment style. Our attachment style can affect everything in life because relationships are such a core part of the human experience. It can influence our self-concept and our perceptions and determine the behaviors we choose.

If you notice repeated patterns in your relationships, become curious about what early dynamics you may be repeating. You were helpless and dependent as a child when you first adapted to your caregivers and formed your attachment style. But right now, you are an adult who has the power of awareness and conscious responsibility, so you can choose to re-work those patterns into something that helps you connect to others in the ways you want to.

CHAPTER 6

How To Reparent Your Inner Child

What you'll learn in this chapter: what your inner child is, how it affects your life as an adult, and six ways you can begin meeting needs that originally went unmet in your childhood.

The theory of the inner child (originally introduced by psychotherapist Carl Jung) rests on the idea that right now, we are all every age we have ever been. As we grow, we add more layers onto our psyches, but at the very core is still the little child we once were. The inner child was once vulnerable and impressionable, and during its earliest experiences with caregivers, its emotions and core beliefs were put in place.

Depending on our earliest childhood experiences, that inner child may be feeling alone, afraid, hurt, or confused. Resolving and healing this pain is what inner child work is all about. By going back to "reparent" ourselves, we put to rest unresolved issues from the past and free ourselves to engage with the present in a more whole, happy, and healthy way.

What do you think your inner child would say to you if it could speak?

Would it cry or throw a tantrum?

Play and be carefree?

Ask for reassurance?

You may never have considered actively engaging this emotional, unconscious part of yourself, but doing so may be one of the most powerful forms of self-therapy you'll ever try. That's because when your inner child is happy and well, you are able to move on in life with more energy, creativity, authenticity, and contentment.

Though your childhood is over, its effects can live on in the present in the form of learned behavior and attitudes. For example, if we learned in early childhood that the world was an unsafe place and that it was useless to ask others to meet our needs, we may grow up to be quite pessimistic and independent, never quite trusting others.

We may see this childhood pain reflected in all our adulthood relationships—that is, until we can go back to that inner child and resolve the issue ourselves. The idea is that ignoring or repressing this pain won't make it go away. It is only by acknowledging, accepting, and healing it that we move on.

If you're wondering whether this kind of work is difficult, scary, or time-consuming, well, it can be! It's also usually something that is done with the help of a trained therapist. However, you may be surprised at just how intuitive these exercises are and how much you enjoy them once you try them for yourself.

Reparenting Yourself

In the seventies, Dr. Lucia Capacchione used art therapy to help her clients access and heal their inner children. The goal is to reclaim and reconnect with parts of yourself that have been neglected, much like the process for shadow work described above. The principles are simple because they are not all that different from the way we parent children normally: by making sure they feel loved, safe, valued, and seen.

When, how, and how often you do the following techniques and exercises is up to you. Try them when you're feeling emotional, overwhelmed, or confused. At times like these, there's a good chance your wounded inner child has been activated, so it's an opportunity to step in and engage with them directly. Alternatively try them daily, either in the morning or evening as part of your everyday routines, or incorporate them into other techniques like journaling and visualization.

Reparenting yourself can be summed up very simply: **it's the act of recognizing what needs went unmet for your childhood self and committing to giving that to yourself, right now in the present.**

This idea alone can be liberating. It's never too late to give yourself what you once needed, and the results can be miraculous! If adult problems stem from unmet childhood needs, then meeting those needs in the present has the effect of releasing us from that childhood pain and allowing us to move on, healed.

Here are some practical exercises to try for yourself. Be patient, be kind, and be creative because your inner child is just that—a child. That means they're unique, and what they need most is love and understanding.

Prompt 1: Meet Your Inner Child

Center yourself with a few deep breaths, close your eyes, and try to imagine yourself as a child. See the younger you. What do they look like, what are they doing, and how are they feeling? Relax and let images bubble up for you. Do any particular conversations emerge, or are you reminded of any particular events or memories? Imagine what your inner child is saying or asking for.

If you like, imagine introducing yourself to them. A great way to do this is to find old childhood pictures to jog your memory and give you a visual anchor. "Hello, I'm you but older. It's nice to meet you." Try not to self-censor or judge what comes up for you (i.e., don't tell yourself, "This is silly").

Prompt 2: Start a Dialogue

You want to earn your inner child's trust and let them know that you want the best for them. In your visualization, avoid barging in to tell that inner child what to do, or judging them. Instead, let them speak for themselves in an open-ended dialogue.

Write a letter from your childhood self to your adult self, or vice versa. Remember that facts and details don't matter—feelings do. No perception or perspective is wrong, and you are not on a fact-finding mission.

Simply ask, what did you miss out on as a child? What did you need to hear? What did you wish the adults around you could have provided for you? Then listen with a kind and open heart to the answers that emerge.

Prompt 3: Connect the Past with the Present

Inner child work can take time. To process the past, look for recurrent emotional themes in the dialogues you have with your inner child. Then ask yourself if you feel similarly now as an adult. Can you see any connections or patterns linking the present with the past?

A good idea is to ask, "In what ways did I have to adapt as a child to survive not having my needs met?" Look at your adult life and see if you can identify that learned pattern. For example, as a child, you might have had an insecure attachment style. This led you to adapt by creating a certain core belief about yourself: "If I am perfect and serve everyone's needs, then I can be useful to people and they won't abandon me."

Looking at your adult life, you can see how this core belief impacted your relationships. Now you have a reason to let go of this ingrained pattern and start to engage with others in healthier, more authentic ways.

Prompt 4: Give Yourself Now What You Needed Then

You can come right out and ask, "Inner child, what do you need?"

You could then ask the adult version of yourself to step in and parent the child version of yourself. Do this by:

- Visualizing an encounter with your inner child—for example, in a guided meditation.
- Writing a letter to your inner child to reassure them.
- Writing down or rehearsing a dialogue—try using the Gestalt empty chair technique.
- Literally giving your inner child a little gift or taking them somewhere special. For example, if you felt that your creativity was dismissed as a child, you could go buy some craft supplies and gift wrap them for your inner child. "This is for you—I can't wait to see what you create!"
- Using the insight you gain from a dialogue with your inner child, agree to make changes in your life that reflect your commitment to healing that most vulnerable part of yourself. For example, you may set new boundaries at work, book a long-overdue doctor's appointment, or enjoy a little self-care.

Prompt 5: Use Affirmations

Depending on what your inner child most needed to hear growing up, craft a few sentences that affirm your love and compassion for them:

"You belong."

"You deserve love and respect."

"You are safe."

"You are great just the way you are."

"It's okay to play, to explore, and to express yourself."

"There is enough, and you are enough."

Say these affirmations to yourself whenever you remember. Try writing them at the top of each page of your journal or weave them into meditations and visualizations where you talk to your inner child. By doing so, you are gently re-writing the script you learned all those years ago.

Back then, you were small, defenseless, and completely dependent on your caregivers. But now, as an adult, you are stronger, more self-aware, and able to consciously choose whether to hold on to these self-limiting beliefs or create something better.

Prompt 6: Go on a Playdate

This may feel awkward at first but may be the easiest activity of all. Your inner child loves to play and have fun! So, dedicate some time in your schedule to letting them do just that. Forget what you *should* be doing and just be creative, playful, and light. Have ice cream on top of your cereal if you want to, run as fast as you can through a field, paint faces on rocks you found on the beach, or sing at the top of your lungs without a care for what it sounds like!

For just a moment, put down your burdens; let go of shame, guilt, and anxiety; and reconnect with that childlike part of you that is brimming with optimism, hope, and possibility.

CHAPTER 7

Rewrite the Story of Your Life

What you'll learn in this chapter: that you are the author of your own life, and that it's never too late to rewrite the story.

When you practice self-therapy and re-parent your inner child, you are doing something special: re-writing your life script.

> "I'm so shy; I could never do something like that."
>
> "I was a wild child!"
>
> "I'm pretty unlucky."
>
> "I'm not a math person."
>
> "Women always leave me eventually."

Every time you repeat statements like the ones above, you reveal the unconscious narrative you have taken on for your life. A self-narrative is exactly like a movie script, telling us the role we play and what kind of story we're living. The thing is, although the script may feel like it's written in stone, it isn't—it was put there by our life experiences and can absolutely be changed. But first, we need to be aware of the fact that we are playing out that script in the first place.

Our self-perception can become so automatic and ingrained that we don't see it anymore and simply assume it's fact. We may have been given a narrative as children when we were too young to really understand it, either by our caregivers or society at large, and then internalized that perception and took it on as our own.

In your narrative, you may be the villain, the hero, or the victim. This narrative shapes everything in your life—how you engage with others, how you feel about yourself, your identity and sense of purpose, your choices and how you interpret events—EVERYTHING! So, if you change the narrative, everything else changes, too. Your entire life can be transformed if you can transform the story that your life runs on.

This is where narrative therapy can help. Devised by therapist Michael White, narrative therapy is a way of consciously reclaiming your life's meaning. Instead of living *inside* the script, you step *outside* of it and look at it objectively. Narrative therapy tells us:

- We are all unique, and our experience and perception matters. We are enough as we are.
- We don't need to blame or point fingers; the idea is to understand and take ownership of stories,

not condemn them.

- We are not our thoughts, and we can externalize our problems. Our stories can change.
- We are each the experts on our own lives, and *we* are the authors.

There are many useful narrative therapy techniques out there, but one exercise is especially suited for those wanting to practice self-therapy. The My Life Story exercise is based on the principles of narrative therapy and encourages a holistic perspective on your past and present.

The goal is to create an outline of your life that does not revolve around negative memories and pain as much as moments of intensity or growth. By doing so, you cultivate a broader, richer perspective of your life. When we internalize a narrative, we tend to pay more attention to evidence that confirms our beliefs, thus forming a self-fulfilling prophecy. We also tend to exaggerate the negative while overlooking the positive. The My Life Story exercise works to counterbalance this tendency.

My Life Story Exercise

Step One

Begin with a title (and maybe a subtitle), something that you feel captures the essence of your life. For example: "*To the Top of the Wrong Mountain, a story by Sarah Jones.*"

Step Two

Write at least six chapter titles that reflect significant moments in your life history. Focus on life stages or key pivotal events. Then, write one or two sentences to describe each chapter.

For example, "Chapter 4: The Work Tunnel. *For four years, I worked hard on that PhD, and when I came up for air, I realized that my whole life had changed around me while I was stuck with my nose in a book. Still, I relished the fact that during that period, I seemed to have been christened The Clever One.*"

Continue with all the chapters.

Step Three

Write the final chapter of your life, which includes future dreams, aspirations, goals, and a game plan. This chapter should be longer and more detailed than the others because it is closest to the present and will likely contain themes and issues that are most relevant to you right now.

For example, you could write, "Chapter 10: Finding My Truth. *In the future, I learn more about my own values and make my life according to what I want rather than what is conventionally deemed 'successful.' I find my happily ever after—on my own terms!*"

Step Four

After writing the final chapter, you can go back and add more sentences to the earlier chapters if you would like, but it's not necessary. Remember that this exercise is not about accurately documenting memories or creating a biography for someone else to read. It's more about making an outline or framework to help you identify patterns and gather the emotional checkpoints of your life.

To help you reflect, try using these questions:

- Are there any recurring themes, symbols, or ideas in my chapters?
- Is there a progression or development across all these chapters or events?
- Does the story fit with how I think of myself today? Does it align with how other people view me?
- Is there anything about myself that I used to think or believe but no longer do?
- What do I want to change about my story moving forward? How would I prefer to think of myself?
- If I were rewriting this story, how would I do it?
- Where did this story or this theme come from? When did I first start thinking of myself this way?
- What chapters need to be added in order to bridge the gap between today and the final conclusion?
- Are there different ways to interpret or understand these events? Can I look at them through a different lens now that they are in the past?

For some people, overarching narrative themes become clear when they are made visual—for example, in a diagram. Another way to do the above exercise is to draw out a map or graph of your life so far. Put time along the x-axis, and emotional intensity or happiness/ well-being on the y-axis.

Now, as you move through your life, chart the "beats" or main events where things changed. For example, the line may go up sharply after your marriage, but then, after an illness or financial trouble, drop down again. Sometimes, seeing everything on one page can reveal patterns that look so obvious in hindsight but were nevertheless hidden from your awareness.

For example, you may notice that every single one of your major life transitions has centered around the ups and downs of romantic relationships. Seeing it all laid out this way gives you the insight that you have been unconsciously defining your identity and self-worth according to your relationship status.

Narrative therapy is a post-modern approach, which means that one of its principles is that there is no underlying "objective reality" and that our memories, our self-concept, and our stories are all social and psychological constructs. However, that doesn't mean we cannot gain more insight by finding a "trusted editor" as a second pair of eyes.

If you have a close friend or confidante, you might choose to run your story past them to see what they think. They may be able to spot things that you've missed (if there's something in your shadow, for example, you may unconsciously omit it). They may also prompt you with alternative explanations or suggest a point in your story that doesn't align with their perception of you.

It's up to you to decide what to do when you encounter these discrepancies. It may be that if everyone sees you differently from how you see yourself, you ultimately reject those perceptions and lean into your own. Or it may be that you are able to accommodate their perspectives and let them enrich and balance your own.

What ultimately matters is not the story per se, but the fact that you are consciously engaging with the story *as its author*, not merely a mindless enactor.

Ask for feedback with the understanding that it may be difficult to hear, but also that you don't necessarily have to take it as gospel. Your life is one hundred percent unique, and it's your responsibility to define yourself in a way that aligns with your values and deepest truth. That said, we are all growing and evolving, so don't be afraid to learn something from others, to let them help you see blind spots, or to admit when you've taken too narrow a view on things.

As you can imagine, narrative therapy takes a little bravery, honesty, and creativity. But if you can, it's a great way to take control over your life and start living the story you want to live.

Takeaways

- To better understand how you are, it's worth understanding your early childhood experiences. Your attachment style becomes the model on which all your subsequent relationships are based, and it influences your self-concept, core beliefs, and behavior. If our needs were met by primary caregivers, we develop a secure attachment style and healthy attitudes toward intimacy. However, if our needs were not met or met poorly, we may develop insecure attachment styles.

- There are three insecure attachment styles: ambivalent (where care was inconsistent and we end up too "clingy"), avoidant (where care was lacking and so we overdeveloped our sense of independence, shunning intimacy), and disorganized (where abusive early dynamics created a chaotic attitude toward relationships).
- We can improve our relationships by consciously challenging old patterns, seeking out positive role models, and paying attention to our emotional intelligence and nonverbal communication.
- We can resolve many past issues by re-parenting the inner child. The inner child is the younger version of yourself that still lives on in the present. Reparenting is the act of recognizing what needs went unmet for your childhood self and committing to giving that to yourself right now in the present. Dialogues, affirmations, and playdates can also help!
- Narrative therapy tells us that we are not our thoughts, we can externalize our problems, and stories can change. Use the My Life Story exercise to become aware of overarching patterns and themes in your life. Plot out your life as a story,

but reflect on ways you might like to change that story. A trusted "editor" could also provide feedback and help you think about different ways to frame or reframe your life narrative.

PART 3

Thoughts Are the Code That Programs Your Life

CHAPTER 8

Identify and Change Your Core Beliefs

What you'll learn in this chapter: what your core beliefs are, where they come from, and what you can do to gently challenge them.

The underlying assumptions we have about ourselves, others, and the world in general are known as **core beliefs**.

They are "core" in that they are so deeply ingrained, they may feel like a part of us, like our own name. In the previous chapters, we've already encountered some examples of these, as well as seen how they can stem from early childhood experiences.

Core beliefs emerge in childhood when we learn to interpret the world around us based on our connections with caregivers and our personal experiences. While these mental shortcuts can be beneficial in many circumstances, they can become ingrained patterns of thought, feeling, and behavior that are ultimately self-sabotaging.

If you've ever felt caught in a habit that you can't seem to break, or stuck with a behavior you'd like to change (such as addiction or poor communication), you've probably had a core belief working behind the scenes. For example, in your self-therapy journey, you might have gradually come to recognize a pattern of undervaluing yourself. Digging into it, you see a core belief at the center of it all: "I am not as worthy as other people."

Once you identify this core belief, you see how it manifests itself everywhere—in negative self-talk, in choices that keep you playing small and avoiding risk or exposure, and in relationships with people who seem to unconsciously agree that you are not worth much!

Identifying your core beliefs and assumptions is critical because it allows you to establish the connection between your beliefs and how you're feeling in each passing moment. This insight allows you to take a step back and consider the problem from a different perspective. You get to ask yourself, "Wait, is this how I want to approach this moment? Do I want to keep playing out this tired old loop, or do I want to choose something different?"

A big part of cognitive behavioral therapy (CBT) is learning how to identify and challenge your core beliefs so that limiting perceptions can be reshaped and you can live the life you want to live, experience more happiness, and fulfil your potential. *A core belief is like an internalized "rule" that guides the creation of your personal narrative. We behave in ways to confirm these rules,* i.e., if we encounter something that affirms it, we cling to that and focus on it, whereas if we encounter something that disproves our belief, we dismiss it.

The more we affirm a belief, the more entrenched it gets, which is why it can take time and effort to challenge. Ultimately, we interpret everything through the lens of this belief. If we believe, for example, that we are unworthy as people, when someone smiles at us on the street, we may think, "I wonder why they're laughing at me?" Or perhaps we don't even notice their smile in the first place.

Core beliefs can vary in both their accuracy and their usefulness—our goal in self-therapy is to transform our unconscious, maladaptive, and inaccurate core beliefs into alternatives that genuinely support our wellbeing and growth as people. We can't do this, however, if we're unaware, or unwilling to gently challenge what we "know." We need to constantly remind ourselves that **core beliefs are not facts**. They are just thoughts and ideas that we have repeated so often that we believe them to be true.

Core beliefs can create negative automatic thought patterns. Therefore, when we challenge these so-called "cognitive distortions," we gently loosen the core belief and give a healthier alternative the chance to take root instead.

Let's return to our example core belief—"I am not as worthy as other people"—and see how it inspires negative thought patterns.

1. **Early experiences** – as a child, your father compares you unfavorably to your siblings, and you are routinely interrupted or dismissed since you are the youngest child.
2. **Core belief** that arises to "explain" this painful feeling and help you survive it—"For people to treat me this way, I must be inferior somehow. I must be worth less than others."
3. **Critical incident later in life** – the loss of a job.
4. **Automatic cognitive distortion** – "I lost my job because I'm the worst employee and they all hate me and think I'm stupid. I won't get another job because I'm worthless."
5. **Consequences of those thoughts** – low self-esteem, depression, guilt, shame, and the inability to seek out new work because of the assumption that you will only be rejected anyway. Perhaps even physical symptoms like insomnia and addictive eating.

This sounds dramatic, but core beliefs can also be set up in subtler, seemingly innocuous ways. For example, if you routinely expressed doubt and fear to your caregivers, and they said, "Oh, don't be silly! There's nothing to be afraid of. You're big and strong!" their intentions might have been noble, but you still internalized the core belief that it's shameful to be afraid and that to be considered strong, you need to hide how you really feel.

This core belief may play itself out in all sorts of patterns in adulthood. You may get trapped in the habit of never truly expressing yourself to others, never admitting when you need help, and feeling deep down that if others knew how scared you sometimes felt, they'd think you were "silly." One day you could be having an argument with your spouse when you realize the problem: you cannot honestly tell them that you're afraid, so you're expressing anger instead and causing all sorts of misunderstandings.

The general CBT process is as follows:

1. Identify your core belief
2. Ask whether this belief is really serving you in the present
3. If not, challenge the belief, soften it, or invert it
4. Consciously choose to cement this alternative belief by taking action

For example:

1. Core belief is "it's wrong/weak/silly to feel or express fear"
2. This belief is making your relationships feel shallow and inauthentic; you don't need or want it anymore.
3. You decide to challenge it by inverting the core belief ("expressing your true feelings takes integrity and strength of character") or soften it ("people may sometimes be uncomfortable with others expressing fear, but that doesn't mean I can't safely share my true feelings with those closest to me").

4. Action: decide in the moment to make small steps to admitting fear and doubt. Is it really so bad as you predict? Do people respond as you assumed they would?

The "Downward Arrow" Technique

Here's another strategy that will help you uncover and rework automatic thoughts that are no longer serving you. Remember, of course, that not all enduring, fundamental beliefs about yourself are harmful—but if you find that the cost of this belief is too high, you can change it.

Step 1: Pick a situation that generates negative feelings for you—for example, public speaking.

Step 2: Identify the thoughts that this situation encourages—for example, "I'm weird and awkward and people can tell."

Step 3: Now ask, **what does this negative thought actually *mean* to you?** "It means I have failed to live up to people's expectations of me." You could also ask, "If this were true, why would that be so bad?"

Now, continue asking the questions from step 3.

"If I don't live up to people's expectations of me, why would that be so bad?"

Answer: "Because then they'll disapprove of me and judge me."

"And what does that mean to me?"

"It's means that I don't belong."

"And what does that mean to me?"

"That I'll be a bad person."

And that's it—your core belief: *In order to be a good person, I need to behave like other people.*

You may need to dig a lot, or your core beliefs may be close to the surface, but keep going until you hit something that feels like a deep, fundamental "rule" on which your life is based. Core beliefs tend to fall into three categories: ideas about yourself, ideas about other people, and ideas about the world. Some common ones include:

- I am defective somehow
- I only have worth if other people like me
- The world is an unsafe place, and you can't trust anyone
- I am fundamentally unable to cope
- Life is unfair
- I can only relax if I have total control
- The course of my life is determined by other people's choices

Once you've identified core beliefs, now what? Continue to gently challenge them, invert them, or soften them. The idea is to replace what is automatic, unconscious, maladaptive, inaccurate, and irrational with something that is deliberate, conscious, helpful, accurate, and rational.

Tip 1: Soften Absolutist, All-or-Nothing Language

If you discover words like *never, forever,* and *everyone,* or strong words like *hate, impossible,* and *failure,* try to rephrase them to make them more nuanced and less black and white.

"I always mess up." Do you really? Always? It's probably more accurate to say that sometimes you don't achieve what you want, but that you also have some things to be proud of, and not being perfect doesn't mean you can't learn or try again and do better next time.

Tip 2: Face Your Fears

Cognitive distortions and negative self-talk often revolve around catastrophic thinking—for example, "If I lose my partner, I'll never find anyone else again, and I'll be lonely and miserable for the rest of my life." You create suffering for yourself because you are assuming the worst possible outcome. But *even if this did happen,* is it really so bad? And is it really true that you couldn't cope with it?

Imagine you really did lose your partner and never dated again. Is it true that a partner is the *only* path to happiness in life? Is it really the end of the world? If you face the absolute worst possible outcome, you'll often find that you are exaggerating how bad it is and underestimating your own ability to handle it. The truth is, you will most likely find someone else. But even if you didn't, well, even this outcome is manageable—it may even be preferable!

CHAPTER 9

The ABCD Model

What you'll learn in this chapter: how to use the ABCD model to identify and re-engineer your ingrained thought patterns and cognitive distortions.

Albert Ellis, one of CBT's pioneers, devised the popular ABCD model, which is a classic cognitive behavioral therapy (CBT) technique and one we can make use of in self-therapy. When used correctly, Ellis's approach can help us address a wide range of emotional issues, including anger, depression, or anxiety.

In ABCD,

A stand for **Activating Event** ("trigger").

B stands for **Belief System** (how you interpret your trigger, whether a core belief is at play or not).

C stands for **Consequences** (the emotional and behavioral consequences that result).

> **D** stands for **Dispute** (where we examine, challenge, or reframe our underlying core beliefs, assumptions, and expectations).

The ABCD framework is a great way to structure your efforts to identify and change cognitive distortions, and in so doing change your entire life. While the techniques described in the previous sections are good for uncovering deep and lasting core beliefs, the ABCD technique is more suited for everyday thoughts and self-talk.

While it's always good to understand the deeper emotional and psychological roots of your self-concept, you can also make strides by dealing with cognitive distortions purely on the cognitive level. In fact, many people think of CBT this way—with your brain being a kind of computer and your thoughts being the programming that results in certain emotional and behavioral outputs.

Change the program, change the outputs!

Our minds work so fast that our responses can seem automatic at times. The ABCD model helps us slow things down and take control. We can run through the acronym in the heat of the moment or do a kind of "thought postmortem" after the fact, when we're trying to understand why things happened the way they did. At first, reflecting on events that have already passed may be easier, but with practice, you should be able to start noticing certain thought patterns as they occur.

To begin using the ABCD model, simply run through each of the four letters of the acronym in turn. The magic happens at D, dispute, where you give yourself the chance to act and choose a different way forward for yourself. Many people find the process very calming and grounding, and it can certainly help you dial back strong emotions and see a more sensible, clearer, and simpler way forward.

Here's how.

Get a journal or pen and paper and start making notes (if you're doing this process in the moment, you will obviously frame this process in the present tense and do it somewhat quicker, without writing anything down).

Step 1: Start with the Activating Event

> *What happened?*
>
> *What is the event, thought, feeling, gesture, situation, or dynamic that triggered the present situation?*

Bear in mind that a trigger can be *anything,* from **external** events to **internal** sensations, such as:

- The smell of the tobacco your grandfather used to smoke.
- Being in the car.
- Having to be appraised and graded by superiors.
- Seeing a particular kind of violence in a movie.
- The memory of something that happened in school thirty years ago.

- Feeling sick or unwell.

Step 2: Identify Your Beliefs

What are you saying to yourself about this trigger?

What is your interpretation of events?

What style of thinking or cognitive distortion are you applying?

What core belief is activated?

Remember that this can be lightning fast and so automatic you don't give it a second thought. You might smell tobacco, be unconsciously reminded of your grandfather, and suddenly find your thoughts running away with you, leading to the belief, "I am alone in this world." Or the thought could be a knee-jerk, "I never told him how much I loved him; it's my fault."

Step 3: Identify the Resulting Consequences

What do your thoughts and beliefs make you feel?

How do you behave, given your thoughts and beliefs?

What does this thought or belief imply, cause, or bring about for you?

In our example, the thought, "I am alone in this world," triggered by the smell of tobacco, could cause a feeling of sadness or despair. The thought, "I never told him how much I loved him," could lead to feelings of guilt, remorse, and regret.

On the other hand, consequences are not just feelings.

A consequence can also be a behavior, a decision or choice, or even an adjustment to your attitude or self-concept.

Though not much appears to have changed on the outside, you may quietly make an adjustment to your self-concept to reflect and accommodate your belief, such as, "I always let people down."

Step 4: Dispute the Belief

Once you've explored these beliefs in detail, it's time to challenge your thoughts, beliefs, and resulting consequences.

> *In what ways can you adjust your belief?*
>
> *Can you make it softer, more rational, more accurate, or more useful?*
>
> *Is there a more realistic alternative?*

Having followed the ABCD process, you're probably well aware of how bad it can feel to hold certain thoughts and beliefs. But now is the time to try out something that feels better. Pay attention to how alternative possibilities *feel*—it's not just about finding something that is more rational and realistic. It's also about finding a perspective that feels comfortable and positive. Something that will inspire and enable you to take positive action.

For example, the ABCD process can show you how limiting and self-sabotaging it is to keep beating yourself up for not properly saying goodbye to your grandfather before he died. It simply isn't rational to keep regretting a thing that can't be changed, and it's not exactly fair to carry that guilt forever.

So, you reflect and write down an alternative: "I loved my grandfather and he knew that. I'm not perfect, and I could have treated him better while he was alive, but I can always honor his memory right now by choosing to remember the fond memories instead and not be so hard on myself."

Here are a few more simple examples:

Example 1

Activating event – finding out that two friends have spent time together without inviting you.

Belief – "Maybe they're both talking about me."

Consequence – Feeling suspicious, left out, and hurt; withdrawing socially; and being a little aloof the next time you encounter them.

Dispute – There's no reason to think that two friends spending time together is in any way a problem. There are many benign and reasonable explanations for why they didn't invite you. New alternative thought: "I can trust that my friends like and appreciate me."

Example 2

Activating event – A receptionist has just been rude to you.

Belief – "Nobody knows the meaning of service in this country anymore."

Consequence – Feeling powerless, angry, and apathetic, as well as tempted to be rude in return.

Dispute – This receptionist *is* rude, but not every receptionist in the entire country is rude. In any case, getting angry won't help the situation, so there's no point raising your voice and putting her on the defensive.

The real power of this technique comes in the final step, where we are given the chance to consciously choose something different. Now, just because you completed the process and wrote it down doesn't mean that you won't encounter the same automatic thought again, or that the core belief is gone forever.

You unlearn distorted thinking in exactly the same way as you learned it: slowly, day by day, over a long period.

The good news is that every time you become aware of your triggers and notice your response and the way your core beliefs influence your feelings and behaviors, you weaken old patterns and strengthen new ones. But that does mean that you have to be patient and consistent and not get too discouraged if you cannot make an overnight transformation.

Though you don't have to write down your ABCD process, it's a good idea to keep a kind of "thought journal," at least in the beginning, for a few reasons:

- By writing, you slow your thought process down and give yourself less of a chance to slip into default unconscious patterns.
- You collect a log of triggers, behaviors, and consequences, which will show you overarching themes and patterns over time. This can yield incredible insights.
- With practice, you will learn to better recognize triggers and your responses to them until they disappear completely. You'll know the process is working when you're able to say, "Aha! I've seen this trigger, and I can see myself going down that path. But I feel strong enough to choose my alternative belief, instead."

CHAPTER 10

The Triple Column Technique

What you'll learn in this chapter: a simple but useful technique for homing in on your cognitive distortions—the filters you place over objective reality.

What you tell your mind to believe, it believes.

That means if you fill your mind with negative self-talk all day every day, your life will be shaped by that negativity. So many of us think that our inner self-talk is just a neutral narrator casually perceiving events, but really, our inner talk *shapes* our perception, and then our perception works to confirm what we have already decided we believe.

The goal is to become aware of our self-talk and be more discerning about the effect it is having on our perception and therefore our lives. We don't have to take our self-talk's word for it! Instead, we can check to see whether it's distorted, and ask the more conscious, healthier, and more realistic part of us to *talk back* to that negative self-talk and correct those distortions.

This is what the triple column technique can help you do. Using this technique, you can zoom in on cognitive distortions so you can moderate them. Here's a step-by-step process.

Step 1: Create Your Table

On a piece of paper, draw two lines to make three columns, each labeled:

1. Automatic thoughts
2. Cognitive distortion
3. Rational response

Step 2: Write Down Your Self-Critical Thoughts

In the first, far left column, begin by writing down the negative self-talk you've become aware of. This will be a mix of core beliefs, emotions, expectations, assumptions, biased, guesses, judgments, interpretations, and reactions. For example:

This is a complete, total disaster.

This always happens.

I'm to blame.

I bet he's angry with me.

I was supposed to do better.

Step 3: Identify Cognitive Distortions

Some of your thoughts may be positive, hopeful, inspiring, kind, and rational. But if you're reading this book, chances are your self-talk tends to be more critical and negative! In the middle column, for each of the thoughts you noted in step 2, identify any cognitive distortions that apply (more on this in just a moment).

Step 4: Explore Rational Alternatives

In the final column, try to find more accurate, useful, and positive alternatives for each thought. Now, it's important that this alternative thought is still realistic. You don't need to tell yourself comforting lies or unbelievable platitudes. You don't need to "cheer yourself up" or pretend that things are better than they are.

So, for example, a good alternative for, "I'm fat and out of shape and completely unattractive," could be, "I have many positive attributes, and if I'm unhappy with my health or appearance, I can always make positive changes." The alternative, "You are the most attractive person to ever live," is just as distorted—plus, you're unlikely to believe it, anyway.

Once you've identified these alternatives, the hard part begins—you need to consistently remind yourself to counter every negative bit of self-talk with a more positive rebuttal. Again, it takes time and practice. In the beginning, you may be quite surprised just how much negative self-talk you engage in!

Let's now take a look at cognitive distortions—which are exactly what they sound like—inaccurate, twisted perceptions that don't properly reflect the reality they are observing.

It's worth noting that having rational and adaptive thoughts won't absolve you from ever having to suffer. But they will ensure that you are not unnecessarily adding to your own suffering with your thoughts. The goal of any CBT-inspired self-therapy is not to be completely rid of negative emotion—that's impossible!—but rather to have a healthier, more mature, and grounded response to life's inevitable challenges.

Here are a few common cognitive distortions:

Disqualifying the Positive

When something positive threatens to disprove a negative core belief or automatic assumption, then the tendency is to discount it.

> "I know I received a positive performance review last week, but that was probably just a fluke. What matters is the fact that my work was questioned this morning. *That's* the more accurate reflection of my professional capabilities."
>
> Rational alternative: *We are all complex individuals who contain both good and bad attributes, and we are okay just as we are.*

Mind-Reading or Fortune-Telling

This is when we act as though we can tell with one hundred percent accuracy what other people are thinking, or that we absolutely know what events will unfold in the future.

> "He thinks I'm an idiot, I know it."
>
> "I can't share my idea because I'll just be shut down."
>
> Rational alternative: *We cannot read minds or predict the future. The only way to be sure is to communicate or wait to see what the future brings!*

Magnifying or Minimizing

Blowing something way out of proportion or minimizing it into nothing depending on what the prevailing core belief requires.

> "I made a typo on page three and that basically means my boss will fire me on Monday, I'm sure of it."
>
> "I wouldn't want to worry those poor doctors with my broken leg. It's really not that bad . . ."
>
> Rational alternative: *The truth usually lies somewhere in the middle of extremes. Whatever I encounter, big or small, positive or negative, I can cope with it.*

Personalization

This is when we interpret events as though they always necessarily connect back to us somehow, making us take on more responsibility, blame, or even praise for things that really have nothing to do with us.

> "My son wouldn't have failed math if only I had pushed him a little more."
>
> "She's in such a bad mood; I wonder what I did."
>
> Rational alternative: *Even though I care, I cannot be responsible for other people's emotions or actions.*

Labeling

This is what it sounds like—putting labels, often harsh ones, on experiences or perceptions. When you label yourself, you're assigning yourself a fixed role in your narrative. The trouble is, this is usually limiting or inaccurate.

> "I'm a moron."
>
> "I could never relax with my OCD tendencies."

Labeling can range from the obvious ("You're an idiot.") to the more subtle ("Well, I'm half-Italian—I'm just hot-blooded."), but in each case, it acts to remove you from spontaneous, conscious choice in the moment and instead makes you behave in automatic, stereotyped ways.

Rational alternative: *I am many things, but in every moment, I can make new choices, and I'm not bound forever to keep making the same choices I made yesterday.*

All-or-Nothing Thinking

This is easy to spot if only you look. Black-and-white thinking poses just two extremes, when reality is usually a lot more nuanced.

"They didn't hire me for the job, so they must think I'm incompetent."

"If it rains on the last day, our whole vacation will be ruined."

"You're with me or against me."

Rational alternative: *There are endless shades of gray between two extremes, and there are usually more than just two options in life.*

Generalizations

One very common cognitive distortion is to over-extrapolate, i.e., to take one isolated instance and assume that this implies something about every other instance, everywhere, at all times. Like so many of the other distortions on this list, the effect is to flatten out nuance, simplify reality, and give us a picture of the world that is easier to manage—the price is that this simplified picture is usually wrong!

"Men just don't care about marriage as much as women do."

"She's a lawyer; don't trust a word she says!"

Rational alternative: *Life is complex. I encounter each situation, person, and event individually. I am always willing to question my biases and be proven wrong.*

"Should" Statements

We may sometimes overestimate our knowledge and assume we perfectly understand the "rules" on which our world runs. That's why we can boldly state what "should" and "shouldn't" happen—and get upset when it *doesn't* happen that way.

We miss out on the fact that we seldom have the perfect and complete information needed to make such pronouncements. When you examine why you believe something ought to have been the case, you may find nothing more than a few flimsy assumptions and expectations that are not really based in reality.

"You are X years old; you should have this all figured out by now."

"This should not have happened."

Rational alternative: *I may have a preference for a particular outcome, but how the world unfolds is largely not under my control. There is no point arguing with reality, but I know that whatever a situation's outcome, I can cope and make choices according to my own values.*

Cognitive distortions are easy to grasp when written on the page, but it takes awareness and practice to identify them in your own life. After all, the most impactful distortions are likely to be the ones that are most entrenched and most invisible to you.

Luckily, we have a flag that signals that cognitive distortions may be at play: every time we feel overwhelmed emotionally, whether that's anger, sadness, anxiety, or confusion, we can stop and say, "What's going on with my thoughts right now? And how are these thoughts making me feel?"

Write them down (there may be many!), identify any distortions, then go in and re-engineer those thoughts.

The next time you encounter the same trigger, the idea is to remember the alternative and deliberately revert to that instead. Yes, it will take time for these updated, more moderate versions to take hold, and at first, they may not feel easy or natural. But with consistent practice, you will find it easier. You will reach a point one day where it is the old, maladaptive thought that feels unnatural, while the more rational one feels better!

CHAPTER 11

Cognitive Defusion

What you'll learn in this chapter: three techniques to quickly gain distance, control, and perspective when you feel overwhelmed by thoughts and feelings.

Identifying core beliefs and using the ABCD model and triple column technique can all feel pretty exhausting!

Especially if anxiety and overthinking are a problem for you, it may seem like all these techniques and models only add to the stress of trying to manage and untangle your thoughts. Even though CBT is NOT about forcefully stopping certain thoughts, it can sometimes feel like you're playing "whack-a-mole" with intrusive, negative, or self-critical thoughts.

If this is the case and you often feel like your head is a big mess of knots and tangles, you might enjoy the approach suggested by ACT, or Action Commitment Therapy. One goal of ACT is not to change, fight, repress, or battle thoughts and feelings. Instead, **we**

change how we relate to those thoughts and feelings. Big difference.

To put it another way, the idea is that the *content* of our thoughts is never the problem. Rather, it's our attitude and *response* to that content that can create trouble for us.

Person A may have the thought, "Nobody loves me," and respond to that thought by completely identifying with it. They focus on it fully, believe it, and allow it to drag them down a rabbit hole of similarly dark thoughts.

Person B also has the thought, "Nobody loves me," but they are not identified (or what ACT calls "fused") with this thought. They don't take this thought as one hundred percent absolute truth.

Person A is experiencing being unloved. Person B is experiencing the *thought* that they are unloved.

Person A is fused with their experience, feeling it as absolute reality, whereas Person B understands that they are in fact just having an experience and that reality and thoughts about reality are not necessarily the same thing.

Person B is practicing cognitive defusion and detaching themselves from their experience rather than identifying with it. No, they are not emotionless robots—the thought, feeling, and experience is still there. The only difference is that they are not lost and drowning in it. They look at thoughts from the outside rather than at the world from inside their thoughts.

They are aware and can notice what is happening to them.

Sometimes, when we **battle** our thoughts, we only end up creating more of the same problem. Importantly, being "fused" this way can entail both clinging to an experience or desperately avoiding and denying it. Either way, we are still being pushed around by the thought! It is our response to the thought that is creating problems, not the thought. So unless we change our response, we stay tangled.

The ACT defusion techniques we will look at below all work because they achieve the following:

- Increase psychological distance from strong experiences, reducing negativity
- Remind us that our thoughts are not the same as reality
- Remind us that we are not slaves to the influence of our thoughts
- Help us stay flexible, open-minded, and creative
- Keep us in the present moment when we can respond to our experiences spontaneously
- Stay connected to our power to choose what we do and how we respond

ACT is essentially a way to develop metacognition, i.e., to **think about your thinking.**

Set aside the content of whatever thoughts, feelings, and experiences you're having and look at them *as thoughts*—are they actually helping you in any way? Are they causing you to suffer? Is this thought in control of you or are you in control of it? Is it helping you achieve the kind of life you want for yourself, or is it getting in the way?

Even if you don't actually answer these questions, the mere fact of asking them puts you in a completely different frame of mind—calmer, more rational, and more proactive.

Defusion Technique 1: "I'm noticing that . . ."

Try saying these words: "I'm noticing that I'm having the thought of/the feeling of/the experience of . . ."

You gain psychological distance. You are not the thought; you are just *having* the thought. If the thought comes, then it will go again. It's just a temporary experience that you can observe in yourself. It's important not to judge or interpret the experience. Your only job is to notice it.

> "I'm having that same old cognitive distortion again . . ."
>
> "I'm experiencing a strong feeling of sadness right now."
>
> "I notice my mind wanting to follow each of these anxious thoughts. I also notice that when I do this, there's an instant tightness all along my shoulders."

Defusion Technique 2: "Thanks, mind."

You are not your mind. Your mind may whir along automatically and generate all sorts of thoughts, which cause an endless conveyor belt of feelings. But your mind is just one part of you, like your circulatory system or your middle toe.

Consider that when you have allergies, your immune system is trying to do its job but has made a kind of error in perceiving something harmful as a threat. The problem is the response itself. Your immune system can be in overdrive, but you are not your immune system, and luckily you know that there really isn't any threat. That's why you can safely take an antihistamine to deal with the symptoms, effectively saying, "Thanks, immune system, but everything's under control."

Similarly, your mind's job is to think, process, plan, create, and so on. Like the immune system, it gets carried away sometimes, though. Overthinking, anxiety, and negative self-talk are not actually helping you in any way, even if they feel like they are. So in these instances, you can consciously thank your mind for trying its best to do its job—and choose not to believe it!

> "Thank you, fear, for trying to keep me safe. I'm going to take a chance, anyway."
>
> "Thank you, mind, for bringing that to my attention. I'll consider it later."

The trick is not to take your thoughts as gospel, and sometimes, even use a little humor or sarcasm. If you like, give your recurrent unhelpful beliefs names and identifies. For example, you can imagine your anxiety as a comically melodramatic panda holding a sign saying, "The end is nigh." You can notice it, smile, and say,

"Thanks, Doom Panda. I know you're trying to help. But sit down and relax because I'm busy living my life!"

Defusion Technique 3: Leaves on a Stream

When we are fused with our experience, it seems to expand and fill all our awareness. For example, we feel anxious and worried, and it suddenly seems like this is how we have always felt, and we can't imagine feeling any different in the future. We forget that sensations and perceptions are *fleeting*—they come and they go again.

The Leaves on a Stream exercise is very simple meditation to try when you feel the relentless onslaught of too many thoughts and sensations. What it helps you do is realize that sensations are not permanent. Too often we prolong suffering because we either cling to or resist certain experiences. However, if we only relaxed and let them go, they would move and flow of their own accord without us having to fight or cling to them.

Here's how to do the exercise:

1. Take a few deep breaths; close your eyes; and imagine a peaceful, calm, and clear stream flowing gently past your feet.
2. Just enjoy this stream and notice how it is always moving—never hurrying or dawdling, but just moving along with ease as it goes.
3. When a thought pops into your mind, imagine taking this thought out of your head and gently placing it on a leaf floating by on the river. Watch

the thought gently bob out of view as the river carries it away.

4. When another thought emerges in you (or the same one!), put it on another leaf and watch it, too, float by.
5. You are not resisting any of these thoughts. You are just allowing them to come and then go.
6. When you are feeling a little calmer, open your eyes again. You can repeat this exercise any time you feel overwhelmed by thoughts and feelings.

If you like, you can combine all three of these defusion techniques into one and make any adaptations you like. For example, you could imagine that there is a tiny person sitting on top of your head, and every time you have a thought, a little party balloon emerges. You imagine the little person tying a knot in this balloon and then releasing it into the air where it floats away until it becomes a pinprick on the horizon.

As you visualize all this, you say things like, "I'm noticing a feeling of shame. Thank you, mind, for this balloon, but I won't need it. Goodbye!" Perhaps you picture each thought as a different-colored balloon, or imagine putting tiny, shrunk-down versions of your problems and worries into the balloons, where they become harmless and inconsequential.

Whichever way you choose to practice defusion, just remember some key principles:

- Gain distance
- Stay present
- See your thoughts *as thoughts*
- Stay flexible and choose not to respond
- And most importantly: **don't fight** sensations; simply let them flow on.

Takeaways

- A core belief is a deep and fundamental assumption or idea that impacts our identity and behavior, as well as the life narrative we create for ourselves. We can transform our unconscious, maladaptive, and inaccurate core beliefs into alternatives that genuinely support our wellbeing and growth as people. In CBT, we identify, challenge, and rework core beliefs. We can identify core beliefs with the downward arrow technique.
- Our goal is to replace what is automatic, unconscious, maladaptive, inaccurate, and irrational with something that is deliberate, conscious, helpful, accurate, and rational.
- The ABCD model stands for Activating event, Belief, Consequences, and Dispute. We can use it to identify and re-engineer your ingrained thought patterns and cognitive distortions. By identifying the four parts, we can discover more rational alternatives to habitual thought patterns.
- Cognitive distortions are like a filter placed over

objective reality. The triple column technique can help us identify and address these distortions. Write down a thought, identify possible distortions, then soften, invert, or moderate that thought and revert to it next time you have that thought again.

- Cognitive defusion is a way to quickly gain distance, control, and perspective when you feel overwhelmed by thoughts and feelings. We suffer not because of our experiences, but our responses and attitudes toward those experiences, i.e., our over-identification with them.
- Defusion techniques include using the phrase, "I'm noticing that . . ." thanking our mind for trying to help and using the Leaves on a Stream meditation to let thoughts flow on without resistance or clinging.

PART 4

Build the Life You Want One Action at a Time

CHAPTER 12

Systematic Desensitization

What you'll learn in this chapter: how to systematically face your fears and break old limiting associations so you can build new ones.

In Parts 1, 2, and 3, you delved deep into your own psyche, carefully considered your core beliefs, integrated your early childhood experiences, engaged your shadow, and reconsidered your personal life narrative.

This kind of work is invaluable, no doubt. However, it's incomplete unless it's combined with deliberate **action** in the world.

Much self-help advice out there takes the reverse approach and starts with goals, actions, and behaviors with the hope that it will inspire positive internal changes. However, you're more likely to succeed if you work "from the inside out" and allow your actions and behaviors to emerge from a strong, healthy sense of self.

Systematic desensitization is an evidence-based

therapy that combines relaxation techniques with gradual exposure to help you overcome a phobia, such as fear of flying, heights, or public speaking. However, the principles and techniques are useful even if you don't have a specific phobia you'd like to challenge.

The power of systematic desensitization is that it allows your inner world to interface with the outer world—it creates an arena where you can literally *test out* your core beliefs, assumptions, biases, and expectations. This real-world practice can be far more powerful than merely talking or thinking about the changes you'd like to make in your life.

Here's how it's practiced: you work your way up through increasing levels of emotional intensity, which explains the other term this technique is known by: progressive exposure therapy. You start with the least intense and consciously and deliberately dial up the intensity.

There are three key processes involved for the process to work:

1. A **hierarchy** of intensity (in the classic case, the emotion in question is fear or panic)
2. Slow and **incremental or graded** exposure
3. Relaxation techniques used to **desensitize** you to progressive levels of exposure

The overall goal of this technique rests on classical conditioning. You create new associations between relaxation and what is normally threatening or frightening. Over time, a stimulus or situation will stop producing the same negative reaction in you as you gradually "teach" yourself a new way of responding.

There are a few different ways to practice systematic desensitization, but here is a simplified approach you can follow on your own.

Step 1: Choose Your Favorite Relaxation Technique

You need to find a way to induce feelings of calmness and control in yourself. There are many ways to do this:

Visualization

For example, closing the eyes and imagining in vivid detail a beautiful, serene place that makes you feel calm, such as a garden or peaceful beach.

Deep Breathing

Slow and regulate your breathing so that your heart rate drops and your nervous system is calmed down and regulated. Take a few deep, slow belly breaths and deliberately imagine yourself relaxing both physically and mentally.

Progressive Muscle Relaxation

Your muscles can access deeper states of relaxation if they tense up first. Lie down somewhere and, moving through the different parts of your body, tense up a muscle for a few seconds, then very slowly release the tension as you breathe and relax fully. Repeat a few times before moving on to the next area, paying close attention to places where tension often occurs: the neck, jaw, and shoulders.

Meditation

The Leaves on a Stream technique above is very calming and focusing, but you can also use other mindfulness techniques such as mantras, chanting, or simply bringing your mind back to the present moment when it wanders.

Step 2: Create Your Hierarchy of Emotions

Next, you need to set up a framework so that you can pair relaxation with those situations, ideas, or phobias that normally trigger negative reactions. This is the "systematic" part of systematic desensitization.

How you do this will depend on what you're trying to achieve. The classical approach to tackle phobias might look something like this:

1. You identify the most frightening level of fear and what that would be—for example, speaking in public in front of a big crowd of people for more than five minutes. This is set at "Level 10."
2. You identify the lowest level, "Level 1," which might be merely imagining talking in front of a crowd of people.
3. You fill in the gaps between Level 1 and Level 10

so that you have progressively more fear-inducing situations, such as talking in front of only two people, or talking to a crowd but for just thirty seconds. There are no rules here—it rests purely on your personal perceptions.

4. For each level, devise a practical, real-world activity. If giving practice speeches to a small room of seated people is at Level 5, then you might sign up for a public speaking course so you can literally do this.
5. You're finished with this step of the process when you have a kind of ladder of progressing intensity.

Step 3: Move through Gradual Exposure

The first thing to remember: **you are in control.** There is no force; you choose how fast you move up the ladder.

The second thing is that as you move through the activities for each level, you need to pay careful attention to pairing your experience with the relaxation technique you chose in Step 1. You are not needlessly exposing yourself to stressful or unpleasant things for the sake of it! Rather, you are trying to break your fearful associations by creating new experiences around that stimulus. Without the relaxation element, you may in fact be reinforcing negative patterns, not breaking them.

The process is simple. Start at Level 1. Let's say this is thinking about your fear—spiders. As you do this, notice your anxiety levels. When they get unmanageable, use your relaxation technique to calm you down again. Keep going.

How do you know when you can progress to the next level? That's easy: when you are comfortable at the current level. So, if you are able to think about spiders comfortably, then you can try Level 2, which is where you look at cute cartoon pictures of spiders.

Again, when you notice anxiety, you use your relaxation technique again. Try to closely pair the relaxation with the exposure. In other words, try to summon up feelings of calm *while* you're engaged in the unpleasant sensation. When you have reached the final and highest level, congratulations—you have cured yourself of your phobia.

You're probably wondering how this technique can be applied to conditions other than public speaking or fear of spiders. Granted, the approach doesn't work for every single issue out there, but as long as you can build in the three components (hierarchy, graded exposure, and desensitization with relaxation techniques), then you'd be surprised how versatile it can be.

Systematic Desensitization Example: Social Anxiety

This could encompass a whole range of behaviors, feelings, situations, challenges, and thoughts. Let's say you're a painfully shy person who has been working on their self-esteem and core beliefs, but realizes that at some point, you have to go into the world and take risks. You construct the following "ladder" of graded exposure and pair each step with deep breathing and visualization.

1. Think about greeting one person in class
2. Think about greeting a group of people in class and striking up a conversation with them
3. Smiling at someone in class
4. Greeting someone in class
5. Greeting a group in class; striking up conversation
6. Smiling at a stranger in the street/ in a supermarket
7. Greeting a stranger
8. Striking up a conversation with a stranger
9. Introducing yourself to a group of strangers
10. Striking up a conversation with a group of strangers

Depending on how you use it, the approach can be adapted for anger management, generalized anxiety, bad habits, or addictions. If you are trying to *create* a new conditioned response as opposed to just getting rid of one, you might choose to use both relaxation techniques and affirmations to cement new core beliefs. For example, if you are trying to develop better eating habits and a healthier relationship to food, you could gradually expose yourself to situations you know trigger certain unwanted behaviors, such as buffets.

The next time you're at a buffet (let's say that's Level 4), you quickly do a visualization where you see yourself calm, happy, and in control, and you also bring out some pre-chosen mantras and affirmations ("I make choices to support my health and wellbeing. I can binge if I want to, but I choose instead to eat in a way that makes me feel good about myself.")

If you have a genuinely stubborn or debilitating phobia or issue, it may be wise to consult a therapist who can at least guide you and set you off on the right foot. Those with more serious PTSD, for example, may not benefit from systematic desensitization. Likewise, you may need some help in setting appropriate targets (for example, it isn't advisable to use the approach to help you become progressively desensitized to things that are in fact bad for you, like an abusive relationship).

Remember that even though the process may be scary and uncomfortable at times, you are always in control, and you can always choose how fast to go, where to go, and when. That's the beauty of self-therapy!

CHAPTER 13

Behavioral Activation

What you'll learn in this chapter: why staying active and engaged in life is so important, and how to create a life that best reflects your deepest values.

The premise of behavioral activation is pretty simple: when you're depressed, you're less active. That means you're not out there in the world, encountering new potentially rewarding experiences. Therefore, you end up more depressed!

Without realizing it, you are stuck in a cycle of low mood and negative feelings. In this situation, staying at home to dwell forever on reflection and "self-therapy" may be precisely the thing that is keeping you feeling bad.

Instead, according to behavioral activation theory, you need to **do something.**

With all this talk of inner children, shadows, and invisible core beliefs and narratives, you could be forgiven for forgetting you have a body at all. But you do, and there is a close relationship with your mood and what you do with that body. While therapy is great, some of the best things you can do for yourself include the obvious: spend time with loved ones, move your body, learn something new, or go on an adventure. By acting, you give yourself the chance to create three important things:

1. Pleasure
2. Mastery
3. Connection

Break the cycle of inactivity and depression by being proactive. Because you're breaking a cycle, though, and because there may be very little initial momentum, you have to take the first step *even when you don't necessarily feel like it.* It's a mistake to think that motivation is needed for action—sometimes it's the other way around, and action inspires motivation!

There are a few components to master when introducing behavioral activation into your life:

Step 1: Monitor Your Activity

You need to first understand your activity levels and patterns, as well as how that affects your mood day to day. To do this, keep a record that tracks what you are doing for literally every hour of your waking life. You might think you already know how you spend your time, but prepare to be surprised. Sometimes, visually seeing your schedule on one page can give you a more accurate and unexpected sense of what you're actually doing with your time . . . i.e., your life!

You can easily create a chart for yourself in Microsoft Excel or simply draw up your own table by hand, leaving enough space to jot down a word or two, such as "watching TV" or "working." You might also like to present the data in different ways and list how many hours go to each activity (a pie graph can be insightful!).

One important thing to do: simultaneously track your mood. For example, you could use a ten-point scale or simply assign a word to each day, like "calm" or "grumpy."

Step 2: Analyze Your Activity

Once you've gathered such data for around a week (more is better), it's time to look at the bigger picture and ask yourself: **are there any patterns between my activity levels and my mood?**

Some more questions to guide your analysis:

> *Which activities were associated with the best mood? And vice versa?*
>
> *Is there any connection between activity level/ intensity and mood?*
>
> *How did you feel on days when you didn't leave the house or talk to another person?*

Depending on your answers, you can now compile a list of activities that you know create good feelings, and a list of those you know that don't.

On your list of Activities that Make Me Feel Good, you might include a daily walk, talking to a friend on the phone, or eating a healthy home-cooked meal.

On the list of Activities that Make Me Feel Bad, you could include a Netflix binge, scrolling social media, or getting out of bed at noon.

The point of monitoring and analyzing your own data is to prove to yourself, to literally *see*, the connection between your activity levels and mood. There may be a few surprises in there—for example, you may discover that talking to friends on the phone makes you feel better, but only certain friends!

Step 3: Reflect on Your Values

You may be the kind of person who says, "My family means everything to me," and yet when you look at how you actually spend your time, you realize that you devote more hours to TV, mindlessly browsing junk on the internet, and shopping than you do spending quality time with loved ones. In other words, your life is not reflecting your deepest and truest values.

Our values are those things that add genuine meaning to our lives. They influence how we engage with others, our priorities, how we see ourselves, and what choices we make. A happy and balanced life is one guided by our values; an unhappy one is where our goals, actions, and priorities have nothing to do with our values.

Take some time identifying what your values are, i.e., your "big why" guiding all your actions. Some examples:

Family life, children, and parenting
Your romantic relationships, marriage, connection
Spirituality
Fun, adventure, new experiences
Education and learning
Personal development, healing
Service, community, charity
Financial success, professional development, career
Creativity
Physical wellbeing and health

Your values can change throughout life, and you may hold several values, each with a different level of priority. As you reflect on your values, though, ask yourself, "**Have I lived my life in accordance with my values?**" Luckily, the previous activities and exercises will have given you additional insight into what really matters to you fundamentally.

Step 4: Activate Value-Driven Activity

Now that you know how you spend your time, what you value, and the degree of overlap between these two things, you can take informed, conscious action to improve. Simply acting isn't good enough—it needs to be activity that speaks to your values. Remember, too, that you might not necessarily feel like it in the moment, but that if you have monitored your routines and identified your values, you *know* that certain activities will benefit you.

Consult your list of Activities That Make Me Feel Good and devise some tasks to try according to your values. Sometimes feel-good activities are exactly the same as value-aligned activities, but sometimes you may have to make some tweaks. Try creating an "activity menu" of options you know you enjoy and which are important. For example:

Yoga
Eating or cooking a good meal
Movie night with spouse
Volunteering
Reading a good book
Taking the dog for a walk
Sports with friends
Enjoying a solo hobby
Tidying the house

Now, don't dive in and try to do every single one of these activities immediately. Instead, just as you did with systematic desensitization, rank the activities from easiest to hardest. Each takes different amounts of energy and yields different levels of benefit. Rank them according to ease, then pick the easiest ones first. This way, you build momentum and work your way up to more intensive activities over time.

Schedule some activities for the coming week, being specific about what you plan to do, when, with whom, and so on.

Finally, an important last step: continue to monitor how you feel. During this week, keep track of both your activity levels and your mood. Note how you felt afterward so that you have enough data to make any necessary adjustments for the week after that.

Step by step, you design your life consciously and in accordance with your principles. You don't just take any old action, but action that is aligned with your values. You may be surprised at just how effective such a data-driven approach can be!

A few tips as you master this strategy:

- Go slow and take baby steps. You want to gradually build up to more activity—doing too much too quickly can burn you out.
- Consider breaking bigger and more energy-intensive tasks into smaller, easier ones first. This makes things much less overwhelming and more manageable.
- Give yourself a reward when you successfully make positive changes, and take time to acknowledge the progress you've made.
- Have self-compassion and don't beat yourself up if you end up procrastinating or canceling activities. At the same time, challenge yourself and don't let yourself get away with saying, "I'm too tired. I'll do it when I'm feeling better."
- Finally, make sure that you're paying attention to tasks that are absolutely necessary and prioritizing those. These are things like showering, filling

an important prescription, or making sure the grocery shopping is done.

- So many of us want to change but lose focus when it comes to making real-world plans and goals. It can be difficult to know exactly how to convert insights from self-therapy work into practical changes for yourself. Behavioral activation is a useful framework that can help you stay organized as you make meaningful, lasting changes to your daily routines.

CHAPTER 14

Behavioral Experiments

What you'll learn in this chapter: how to test out your beliefs and assumptions, and design experiments to help you identify healthier, more rational alternatives instead.

Our final chapter is all about challenging our misconceptions, biases, and assumptions in the best way possible: empirically. "Behavioral experiments" are a way to deliberately examine our beliefs and preconceived ideas and is a big part of self-directed CBT.

In a previous section, we looked at cognitive distortions and how to argue against them. We also closely examined our core beliefs and our personal narratives and how we might challenge these so they can be rewritten. However, the mind is extremely powerful, and many people are masters at fooling themselves, clinging to irrational beliefs despite lacking any shred of evidence!

Behavioral experiments are a great way to get around

our own cognitive illusions and see things the way they really are. An experiment is set up in such a way that we can trust our conclusions to be accurate. Knowing that your beliefs are logical, reasonable, and sound (instead of based on superstition, habit, fear, or assumption) is incredibly liberating.

Conducting a behavioral experiment is not difficult, but it does take some honesty. We have to be willing to drop our filters and be open-minded enough to adjust our perceptions when faced with evidence. We all have mental models that encourage us to focus on what fits our narrative, dismiss what doesn't, and distort everything else so that our prevailing belief is preserved. But we also have the power to challenge those models.

A classic example is impostor syndrome. This is where a person holds a belief in their own unworthiness, and that filter colors everything they perceive. They are unable to acknowledge any praise, awards, or promotions as valid, and instead interpret them in the context of their unworthiness: any achievement must be a mistake, and they'll be found out as frauds any day now.

When we conduct behavioral experiments, though, we put our beliefs to the test, committing to holding only those views that have a basis in reality.

How to Test Your Own Cognitive Hypothesis

A hypothesis is a guess or prediction about what will happen in the future, or a tentative explanation. It's not unlike the "mind-reading" or "fortune-telling" cognitive distortion, though, because often these hypotheses have very shaky foundations, indeed. Using the scientific method, we pose a hypothesis and then test it. We devise an experiment, gather data, interpret that data, and then check to see if the result allows us to reject our hypothesis or not.

There is an infinite number of ways to conduct experiments, but they all follow this basic pattern of hypothesis testing. The next time that hypothesis pops into your head, you can argue against it very effectively—because you have already proven to yourself that it isn't true! What matters is that we approach our hypothesis as scientists do: with curiosity, neutrality, and a genuine desire to understand the phenomenon at hand. That means no shame and blame!

Step 1: Identify the Belief You Want to Test

Try to write this belief or prediction down as a single sentence, looking for things that could be cognitive distortions. For example:

> "I can't join the dance class because other people will laugh at me."
>
> "Everyone at work feels sorry for me."
>
> "If I were to share my true feelings with others, I'd lose everyone."

Step 2: Assess the Strength of Your Belief

This is simple: how strongly do you believe the above

on a scale of one to ten?

You might also like to separate out how much you "believe" it logically versus how much you believe it emotionally. For example, you may know on a rational level that people aren't conspiring against you, but it may nevertheless feel like that sometimes.

Step 3: Design Your Experiment

This part might require a little creativity, but here are three ideas to get you started:

Create a survey. For example, if you think your nose is absolutely hideous and people hate it, then submit your picture to an anonymous forum and ask people what they think—there are places online designed for precisely this purpose! If eighteen out of twenty people didn't even notice your nose, then you have pretty compelling evidence that the hypothesis "my nose is hideous" can be rejected.

Be brave, try it, and see what happens. For example, there's one very obvious way to find out if the hypothesis "I can't join the dance class because other people will laugh at me." Join the class and see! For this to work, though, you need to be brave but also honest.

Try out something new in earnest and avoid self-sabotaging or deliberately interpreting events to support your foregone conclusion. If this sounds extreme, take some inspiration from systematic desensitization and try out a smaller, less risky experiment first, like taking a Zoom dance class where people won't be focusing much on you.

Do the opposite. Sometimes, the only way to test your hypothesis is to stop doing something you have convinced yourself you need to do. For example, the hypothesis "if I don't keep micromanaging my employees, they'll mess up" can be tested by choosing not to micromanage, and waiting to observe if your employees really do mess up. Again, a little courage is needed!

Step 4: Proactively Identify Potential Obstacles

Depending on what you're trying to achieve, plan ahead and make sure that you're giving your experiment the best chance of success. Ask for help if you need it, get advice from others, or see what friends, family, or even a therapist can do to help set up the right scenario. Obviously, you want to avoid any experiments that are dangerous, inappropriate, or liable to backfire.

Step 5: Do the Experiment and Record Your Result

Play out the experiment you've designed and immediately record the results as neutrally as possible. Even better if you can gather hard numerical data about what you find since it's very difficult to argue against cold facts and figures!

In the same way as you identified and adjusted distorted beliefs in an earlier chapter, take the time now to see how your findings compare to your original hypothesis. On the rare occasion, your prediction may actually be confirmed, but it's more likely that you have to make some adjustments. Take the time to literally rewrite the sentence you started with.

> "I can't join the dance class because other people will laugh at me" becomes "Nobody seems to care what others do in a dance class."
>
> "Everyone at work feels sorry for me" becomes "On doing an anonymous 360 assessment, ninety percent of people have no strong feelings about me either way, and ten percent expressed genuine concern about my stress levels but deny feeling sorry for me."
>
> "If I were to share my true feelings with others, I'd lose everyone" becomes "When I share how I feel, people have a range of reactions, but I have not discovered a single piece of evidence that these reactions mean I will be abandoned completely."

Look at the rating you gave your hypothesis in Step 2 and see how you feel now after the experiment is concluded. In most cases, you won't magically reduce this number to zero and be completely free of worries and issues. But you're almost certain to see that number drop.

As you read through the process for behavioral experiments, you might have thought, "Well, that sounds fine, but *my* beliefs and assumptions really are true. I know they are, and I don't need to test them."

It's important to recognize that this is most likely just the voice of fear. If you are terrified at the prospect of being hurt or embarrassed when your worst fears are confirmed, become curious about this fear itself.

Let's be honest: life is complex, and our perceptions are likely to be a *blend* of fact and fiction, truth and illusion. It may in fact be true that you don't have an especially nice nose. But what is *not* true is that your nose is "disgusting," that you are unattractive, that other people notice or care about this feature, and that because of it, you are completely incapable of living a happy and successful life!

Behavioral experiments, then, are not some feel-good way to reassure yourself. Rather, it's about anchoring in reality and embracing your world as fully as you can without distorting biases, expectations, assumptions, and interpretations.

The particular conclusion you arrive at is irrelevant; your sense of *clarity* is the goal. So, after a behavioral experiment, you can change your belief to something a lot more comfortable, mature, and resilient: "I don't have the best nose in the world, but it doesn't seem to matter much because there are so many other great things about me, especially beyond my appearance."

Combined with the other techniques discussed in this book, behavioral experiments can be a powerful way to own your experience, take control, and anchor your perception in the real world.

If this all seems like too much effort, then you can start by simply asking this one question: **do I have evidence for this belief?**

Feelings are not evidence!

If you honestly cannot say you have any hard proof

for a particular belief, then try to understand that you are choosing to believe something that may be completely wrong. A possible alternative: just withhold judgment. Who says you have to always have an opinion, an answer, or a conclusion? Delay making a pronouncement either way.

If you don't have any evidence for or against, there's nothing wrong with saying, "I just don't know." If you were dumped without an explanation, you could easily get carried away with all sorts of reasons for why it happened. But if you ask yourself, "Do I have any evidence for these beliefs?" you will probably find that the answer is *no*.

In this case you cannot do an experiment to find out the "truth," but you can decide not to play a guessing game. Sometimes, the most rational thing we can do is to admit that there are simply things in life we can never understand!

Takeaways

- Systematic desensitization is an evidence-based therapy that combines relaxation techniques with gradual exposure to help you overcome a phobia, but it can also be used to address other issues like social anxiety or anger management.
- First, choose a relaxation technique, such as progressive muscle relaxation, mindfulness techniques, or deep breathing. Then, create a hierarchy of levels, from activities that are least intense or fear-inducing to most intense. Devise an

activity to try for each level. Then, move through each level and gradually expose yourself, using the relaxation technique when your emotions feel overwhelming.

- When you're depressed, you're less active. Behavioral activation is a way to take action and create pleasure, mastery, and connection to others. Take action even if you don't feel like it.
- Start by monitoring your mood and how you actually spend every hour in a single week. Then analyze that activity and represent it visually, looking for patterns and connections between activity and mood. Ask yourself if the way you spend your time reflects your deepest values, whatever they are. Then choose to activate those activities that will speak to your values by scheduling them in, observing the result, and adjusting as you go.
- Behavioral experiments allow you to test out your beliefs and assumptions and design experiments to help you identify healthier, more rational alternatives instead. First, identify the belief (hypothesis) you want to test, assess its strength, design an experiment to test that hypothesis, run the experiment, and then decide whether the results support your hypothesis or not.
- A simple way to bring a more rational mindset to our thought processes is just to ask, "Do I have evidence for this belief?"

Summary Guide

PART 1: GETTING TO KNOW YOUR DEEPER SELF

- No matter who you are, it is possible to improve your life with the same evidence-based techniques used by cognitive behavioral therapists all over the world, i.e., self-therapy can help you live the life you want to live.
- Begin with asking who you are—that is, engaging in self-exploration. With practice, the habit of asking, "What do I notice about myself right now?" will become easier.
- Use Dr. Tom Stevens' six-step approach for cultivating self-exploration: 1) turn on your "inner noticer" and observe yourself without judgment, 2) zoom in on "the problem", 3) follow the strongest emotion, 4) allow yourself to notice any emerging patterns or overarching themes, 5) see what core beliefs are linking everything

together, and 6) use these insights to inspire new, more conscious behavior.

- Carl Jung was the first to talk about the shadow, which is an archetype containing all the unconscious and disowned parts of our psyche. We reintegrate the shadow with patience, non-judgmental acceptance, honesty, and the willingness to face our dark side. We can do this by noticing disproportionate emotional reactions that may hint at the shadow's presence, mindfully embrace our imperfections and weaknesses (humor helps), as well as ask others for their honest feedback on what we can't see in ourselves.
- Gestalt therapy is about understanding how your perception shapes your world, as well as releasing the past so you are more fully available to respond to the present. Some ways to do this include 1) rehearse acts of closure, 2) try the empty chair technique, 3) claim responsibility for your life, 4) shift from the WHY of your experience to the HOW, 5) change questions into affirmations.
- Internal Family Systems posits that the mind is made of many parts in relationship: firefighters, managers, and exiles. Befriend and feel into difficult emotions and normalize them by asking the role they play in your life.

PART 2: SO, HOW DID YOU GET HERE?

- To better understand how you are, it's worth understanding your early childhood experiences. Your attachment style becomes the model on which all your subsequent relationships are based, and it influences your self-concept, core beliefs, and behavior. If our needs were met by primary caregivers, we develop a secure attachment style and healthy attitudes toward intimacy. However, if our needs were not met or met poorly, we may develop insecure attachment styles.
- There are three insecure attachment styles: ambivalent (where care was inconsistent and we end up too "clingy"), avoidant (where care was lacking and so we overdeveloped our sense of independence, shunning intimacy), and disorganized (where abusive early dynamics created a chaotic attitude toward relationships).
- We can improve our relationships by consciously challenging old patterns, seeking out positive role models, and paying attention to our emotional intelligence and nonverbal communication.
- We can resolve many past issues by re-parenting the inner child. The inner child is the younger version of yourself that still lives on in the present. Reparenting is the act of recognizing what needs went unmet for your childhood self and committing to giving that to yourself right now in the present. Dialogues, affirmations, and

playdates can also help!

- Narrative therapy tells us that we are not our thoughts, we can externalize our problems, and stories can change. Use the My Life Story exercise to become aware of overarching patterns and themes in your life. Plot out your life as a story, but reflect on ways you might like to change that story. A trusted "editor" could also provide feedback and help you think about different ways to frame or reframe your life narrative.

PART 3: THOUGHTS ARE THE CODE THAT PROGRAMS YOUR LIFE

- A core belief is a deep and fundamental assumption or idea that impacts our identity and behavior, as well as the life narrative we create for ourselves. We can transform our unconscious, maladaptive, and inaccurate core beliefs into alternatives that genuinely support our wellbeing and growth as people. In CBT, we identify, challenge, and rework core beliefs. We can identify core beliefs with the downward arrow technique.
- Our goal is to replace what is automatic, unconscious, maladaptive, inaccurate, and irrational with something that is deliberate, conscious, helpful, accurate, and rational.
- The ABCD model stands for Activating event, Belief, Consequences, and Dispute. We can use it to identify and re-engineer your ingrained

thought patterns and cognitive distortions. By identifying the four parts, we can discover more rational alternatives to habitual thought patterns.

- Cognitive distortions are like a filter placed over objective reality. The triple column technique can help us identify and address these distortions. Write down a thought, identify possible distortions, then soften, invert, or moderate that thought and revert to it next time you have that thought again.
- Cognitive defusion is a way to quickly gain distance, control, and perspective when you feel overwhelmed by thoughts and feelings. We suffer not because of our experiences, but our responses and attitudes toward those experiences, i.e., our over-identification with them.
- Defusion techniques include using the phrase, "I'm noticing that . . ." thanking our mind for trying to help and using the Leaves on a Stream meditation to let thoughts flow on without resistance or clinging.

PART 4: BUILD THE LIFE YOU WANT ONE ACTION AT A TIME

- Systematic desensitization is an evidence-based therapy that combines relaxation techniques with gradual exposure to help you overcome a phobia, but it can also be used to address other issues like social anxiety or anger management.

- First, choose a relaxation technique, such as progressive muscle relaxation, mindfulness techniques, or deep breathing. Then, create a hierarchy of levels, from activities that are least intense or fear-inducing to most intense. Devise an activity to try for each level. Then, move through each level and gradually expose yourself, using the relaxation technique when your emotions feel overwhelming.
- When you're depressed, you're less active. Behavioral activation is a way to take action and create pleasure, mastery, and connection to others. Take action even if you don't feel like it.
- Start by monitoring your mood and how you actually spend every hour in a single week. Then analyze that activity and represent it visually, looking for patterns and connections between activity and mood. Ask yourself if the way you spend your time reflects your deepest values, whatever they are. Then choose to activate those activities that will speak to your values by scheduling them in, observing the result, and adjusting as you go.
- Behavioral experiments allow you to test out your beliefs and assumptions and design experiments to help you identify healthier, more rational alternatives instead. First, identify the belief (hypothesis) you want to test, assess its strength, design an experiment to test that hypothesis, run the experiment, and then decide whether the

results support your hypothesis or not.

- A simple way to bring a more rational mindset to our thought processes is just to ask, “Do I have evidence for this belief?”